For M on our paper anniversary, with love x

Prologue

GRAND REOPENING BLACK FRIDAY! Every All-mart store across the US has been closed for refurbishment for the last 6 weeks, the media is now full of what are essentially adverts for the grand reopening of all stores on the Friday after Thanksgiving. It's all over the news, Facebook, Twitter - all North American stores will open at 9am Eastern and for the first 3 hours everything in the store will have a price tag of $5, regardless of what it is. Interesting, thought Purdy as she switched apps on her phone, shame there wasn't an Allmart in San Francisco, imagine how much she could stock up on things for $5 each, but then again think of all the people who she'd be fighting with to get the bargains, not really incentive enough for her to venture outside of the city on a holiday, especially when West Coast stores would be opening at 6am.

Purdy woke around 10am on Black Friday and picked up her phone to read the news, it appears that Allmart's advertising had done the trick, there were pictures all over of crowds lining up outside, some waiting patiently for their turn, some requiring police intervention to dampen down any potential riotous behavior. There were also pictures all over of trucks lined up outside of the stores so they could constantly restock. Purdy was impressed at how well organized it all seemed to be. Four hours after the stores had opened and people were still arriving, Allmart had tweeted out that they were impressed with customers' loyalty so they were extending the "sale" from the initial 3 hours to all day or until stock was completely out. Wow, she thought, still not convinced that it was worth her trouble to leave the city.

That was the beginning, if anyone cares to look (and many don't), when things started to change; it can all be traced back to that point in time.

Silicon Valley 5 years later

Purdy sat in the car watching out of the window, thinking about what the day had in store for her. That once endless commute along Highway 101 was a distant memory. The bumper to bumper, start-stop, crazy last minute change in one driver's mind that forced all other drivers to slam on their brakes was no longer a problem here. Since the full adoption of driverless cars in California the traffic now flows freely, everyone equally spaced apart, everyone equally kept at the same speed. Aside from the occasional incident, such as the day the mother duck decided to lead her ducklings across the Southbound carriageway, causing all the autonomous vehicles to safely slow to a stop, traffic jams are a thing of the past.

She watched as she passed the miles and miles of cement jungle, housing the tech companies which enable every aspect of everyone's lives, dotted here along this major artery of Northern California. Exciting and bleak all at once, Purdy thought to herself as she passed quickly by them. Her silent thoughts interrupted by a beeping from her dashboard followed by the chirpy voice of her messaging interface: MESSAGE RECEIVED, FRED: HUNGRY! YOU NEARLY HERE? NEED BREAKFAST! Purdy smiled to herself and spoke back to the interface "Message Fred: yup, be there in 15, hope you survive till I get there". The response was a swift I SUPPOSE I'LL HAVE TO!

She leaned her head back in the seat and closed her eyes for a moment, it felt like it had been a long week and she was looking forward to getting today out of the way so she could enjoy her weekend. A couple of meetings to attend, some contracts to finish up and likely a leisurely lunch with Fred (luckily Fred was always hungry so a great companion for breakfasts, lunches and dinners). She mentally ticked off her to do list and was satisfied it was going to be a good day. Suddenly an urgent beeping broke her train of thought, not the gentle messaging beep she was used to but a more desperate, urgent sound which somewhat startled her. She sat up and looked at the screen in front of her. The car was slowing and pulling over to the righthand shoulder, the urgent beeping was accompanied by an equally urgent flashing icon on the dash.

Puzzled, Purdy stared at the icon trying to decipher what it might be. God forbid they make these things obvious to the lay person. The voice of the interface spoke again: URGENT ENGINE ISSUE, STOP IMMEDIATELY. URGENT ENGINE ISSUE, STOP IMMEDIATELY. Erm, ok, she thought, having no actual control over that, with the car making its own way to the shoulder she felt a little helpless and just sat there until it came to a full stop. The interface spoke again, CALLING TRIPLE A, FAULT DETECTED, DO NOT ATTEMPT TO RESTART VEHICLE. Oh great, she thought, guess I'm going to be stuck here until they send a mechanic vehicle.

Considering what to do, she decided the best plan was to get out of the car and stand somewhere safely away from it. Even if accidents have become less frequent with driver error having been removed from the equation, she still didn't have full confidence that she wouldn't become victim to a runaway vehicle and she'd rather take her chances where she could actually run out of the way if necessary. She picked up her bag and waited for the interface to finish the call to Triple A. Once it was done, she had a message confirming the mechanic vehicle was on it's way and should be there within 14 minutes. Oh well, 14 mins standing in the early morning California sunshine wasn't all bad, she could entertain herself in the meantime. Undocking her phone from the interface, she stepped out of the car, pulling her sunglasses down to cover her eyes from the glare.

Thankfully it was Friday so she was wearing her comfortable Ugg sneakers and jeans. If you're going to get stuck on the freeway, much better for it to happen in casual attire rather than sky high heels and a skirt, just in case running out of the way actually does become necessary. She had alighted the car by the right hand door so as to keep away from the traffic which was streaming steadily past at around 70 miles an hour. Quickly she scuttled to the crash barrier at the edge of the shoulder and stepped behind it.

Better let Fred know she thought to herself. She spoke to her phone "Message Fred: Darn car just stopped, had to call triple A, go eat without me otherwise you'll starve!". The response came almost immediately, before she'd had the chance to look up NOOOOO!! SORRY TO HEAR, HOPE SORTED SOON, I'LL SAVE YOU SOME BACON!. She sent back a smiley face response and looked up to watch the traffic coming along the road.

A seemingly endless stream of perfectly spaced traffic waltzed past her. It was mesmerizing and strangely hypnotic, like watching synchronized swimming or a well choreographed dance, the vehicles effortlessly and invisibly interacting with each other every single millisecond of their journeys. She marveled in the magical technology of it all, and was once again reminded of why she was so attracted to working in this small corner of the world. The amazing technologies which emerge from this pressure cooker of hungry engineers who flock here with their start ups and venture capitalist backers are changing the world on a daily basis and being caught up here in the buzz is so exciting, its hard to imagine working anywhere else would be as exhilarating. She acknowledged to herself that this somewhat made her feel like a nerd as well but she embraced that moniker as a badge of tech-savvy honor.

After a short time she saw flashing yellow lights come over the horizon. She looked at her watch, it had been 13 minutes since she got out of the car, not bad timing she thought, you have to love the efficiency of these automated mechanic vehicles. Before long she would be back on the road after the robotic mechanic had worked its wizardry on whatever had gone wrong with the engine, maybe she should have told Fred to wait for her for breakfast after all.

The vehicle pulled over in front of where her car was stopped and reversed back so it was directly facing the engine compartment. A probe reached out and clipped into the external control pad of the car, presumably this then did a scan to determine what and where the issue actually was. The signage on the side of the vehicle read *AAA, a subsidiary of Allmart*. Interesting, she thought to herself, it seemed Allmart really was trying to diversify in these days of prolific on line shopping. She was staring at the probe again marveling at the technology of it all, watching whilst it performed its magic, when out of the corner of her eye she caught sight of a panel on the side of the mechanic vehicle sliding upward. Ooh, maybe this is some automated robotic arm that's going to come out and fiddle about with things in the engine compartment she thought, fascinated to see it all happening before her.

It was therefore surprising to say the least when a tall figure stepped out of the vehicle from behind the panel. It turns out that the panel was in fact a door and what she thought was an automated, robotic vehicle, was in fact manned. She was slightly disappointed at the revelation and tried to hide her surprise as the figure walked towards her, still a small part of her hoping that it was actually some wonderful new human looking android rather than a real human being whom she would need to interact with. She wasn't very good with new people, being quite shy and mistrustful, choosing to mainly mix with people she'd known forever or only those that she absolutely had to.

In this day and age interactions with strangers were few and far between. Gone were the days of restaurants with actual people making and serving food, automated kitchens and serving hatches had taken their places for the main part, with few exceptions for high end michelin starred chef's places or long established institutions which people had held onto by refusing to allow on line bookings for them to dry up long enough for the owners to consider closing down. Unless you were a foodie and made a hobby out of enjoying fine dining restaurants, rarely would you go to an establishment with real life human beings serving you.

Stores on the whole no longer existed in the real world either, most shopping was now done on line, save for the odd family owned butcher or greengrocer that folks still frequented in real life for nostalgic or novelty purposes. And of course Allmart, which just refused to give in, keeping at least one stronghold in every state allowing people to still come on in and touch before they buy, and sending out email offers to entice folks in on a daily basis. For most, deliveries of on line orders were made by drone and dropped off in the sky hatches that had been installed on the roofs of most dwellings, and usually within hours of the order being made, life had become more efficient, leaving people more free time to work at the jobs they dedicated their existences to.

If something went wrong in the home, it was usually either fixed by connecting it to the manufacturer on line and they would diagnose the issue, fix it if possible or send a replacement if not. If you needed the services of a plumber or electrician that was one of the few times you needed to call out a real human being to come into your house and generally they would come whenever you asked, for Purdy it was preferably while she was out of the house and the home robot dealt with the interaction under the watchful eye of the home camera system. It was rare indeed that Purdy had to deal with a true stranger and rarer still that it happened when unanticipated.

The figure came closer, and it became quite clear that he was certainly not an android, unless they'd come on in leaps and bounds when it came to replicating human skin and fine motor skills, which she was pretty sure she would have heard about. He looked pleasant enough, fairly well dressed and holding a tablet in his hand which he was looking down at scrolling through whatever information he had on there.

"Ms. Sinclair?" he asked as he approached her, his face had no real expression, she smiled at him in the hope he'd return the smile and put her somewhat at ease. His face remained emotionless.

"Yes, that's me" she said trying to sound upbeat and confident even though she was finding the whole thing a little excruciating.

"Hi, my name is Ben" he said, face still emotionless but keeping steady eye contact with her the whole time "We had a call regarding your engine, the car couldn't diagnose the issue on its own so I've been sent as back up in case my mechanic vehicle can't diagnose it either".

That explains that then.

"Oh right. Great... thanks... how long till we find out if the robot can work out what's wrong?"

Finally a small smile spread across his mouth "shouldn't take longer than a couple of minutes." He leant in to her, conspiratorially "Don't let the mechanic vehicle hear you call him a robot, he finds that term offensive".

She was a little taken aback and couldn't tell if he was joking or not... presumably he was but she was finding it hard to read the situation. "Oh! OK... sorry" she mustered.

He looked down at his tablet and started tapping on the screen. Purdy noticed a blinking red light by the camera and felt a little uneasy "erm… are you recording this?" she asked him. Not that she had anything to hide but it still felt weird that he would feel the need to record her in this situation.

He looked puzzled "What? No… What makes you ask that?"

"The red light on your tablet camera was blinking and it was pointed in my direction", she narrowed her eyes, feeling suspicious. He turned the tablet in his hands to look at the camera, there was no red light blinking.

"Hmm" he said "I don't see any light blinking"

"Well no, it's stopped now, hasn't it?"

He eyed her cautiously, he was always wary when going out to meet lone women, he never wanted to put them in a position where they felt uncomfortable with him, for their sake and for his. He made a point again of looking closely at the tablet for a sign of any blinking lights but there were none.

"I think you may have been mistaken? I don't see any sign of a red light…"

"I'm not a moron, you know! I know what I saw…" She realized she was getting a bit worked up but she took her privacy extremely seriously and was terrified at being a ridiculed social media post if she said or did something embarrassing. "Look, I don't know what you're playing at but I'd appreciate it if you didn't film me without my consent, ok?"

He was surprised by her reaction but at the same time felt some empathy towards her, she obviously felt awkward, he saw this all the time these days, people didn't have the chance to mix with total strangers like they once had, so some had lost the ability. Rather than argue he sighed and conceded to her.

"OK, lady, whatever you say"

"Hey, don't speak to me like that!" she was incensed by his patronizing tone, she'd always abhorred being called 'lady' like that as it was only ever done when someone was being dismissive of or talking down to the person they were addressing.

Ben was startled, he was only trying to help this woman, maybe she was some sort of lunatic, just in case he softened his tone.

"I'm sorry, I didn't mean to offend you. Look, I wasn't filming you, I can show you the photo and video files on here if that would make you feel better about it?"

Purdy contemplated the offer. If he was willing to show her then he obviously had nothing to hide so either he wasn't filming her or he had hidden files that the filming would be kept in so she wouldn't see anything anyway. Gosh, she felt paranoid and realized she was showing a little crazy to this stranger, best to let it go she thought.

"No, no. It's fine, I believe you, sorry for making a fuss", she felt the heat of embarrassment in her cheeks and looked down at her feet feeling more and more awkward as the seconds passed.

He went back to tapping on the screen, no sign of that red light, maybe she had been mistaken and it was the sunlight hitting it at an angle that looked like it was blinking. She realized that it was for the best that she'd dropped the subject but felt a bit of a tool for having made a fuss in the first place now.

They continued on in silence, he looking at the tablet and she looking at her feet. She considered small talk but in reality she was still embarrassed at the minor fuss she'd made and couldn't think for a moment what they would have in common to discuss. Finally after what seemed like an age he broke the silence.

"Aaah, that's it!" he grinned to himself whilst she looked up expectantly. He handed her the tablet and pointed to the screen, "all done, if you could just sign with your finger in the box you can get on your way".

She took the tablet from him "er, thanks... so what was wrong with it?".

"Loose wire, would you believe?! Nothing wrong with the engine at all, just the internal electrics weren't giving the right signal to the control panel. But not to worry, he fixed it, shouldn't cause you anymore problems".

Still weird that he called the machine "he" but that explanation was good enough for her. She signed the box with her finger and handed him back the tablet.

"Thanks very much, appreciate your help" she said to him, making a point of making eye contact and giving him a big smile to show everything was ok and she wasn't really a crazy person after all. He smiled back and she felt relieved, however it was not only relief she felt but also a frisson of excitement when they made eye contact, her tummy flipped and that had not happened in a long while. Quickly becoming embarrassed again and not knowing how to deal with the situation she started back towards her car.

"You're welcome!" he called after her. "and don't worry I won't share the photos with anyone else"

She turned so quickly she almost gave herself whiplash. He was stood grinning at her "I'm joking, I'm joking, I promise, there are no pictures!". She realized he was teasing her and her cheeks went pink with shame. She smiled back at him, relieved once again, if he was teasing her about a situation which she had begun to feel mortified about, he obviously wasn't bearing any grudge. She smiled and turned back towards the car again. It was all a bit silly, after all, what pictures could he have possibly got that would be of any interest to anyone anyway? She got into the car and re-docked her phone once again in the interface "Work please!" she said brightly to the interface as the car started up. She pulled the seatbelt across and turned to look out of the window at Ben who was still tapping away on his tablet. He glanced up and she gave him a wave and a smile, he nodded back at her and flashed a grin as the car pulled away. Damn, she thought, he *was* cute but there was nothing she could do about it now though except hope for another car problem and they never happen when you want them to. Which was actually a real shame.

The Daily Grind...

The car pulled up outside the back door of the office. Purdy picked up her phone and exited the vehicle. She tapped the park icon on the phone and the car drove off to find a parking spot as she walked into the building. Being later than usual she hoped that it managed to find a spot in the shade as the early sunshine made it look like it was going to be a warm day, getting back in a hot car at the end of work was never that appealing, if it could park in the shade that made for a nicer beginning to her drive home.

She swiped her pass to open the door. When she first began working here 12 years ago she used to say good morning to the security guard who sat at the desk and helped out if someone had forgotten their pass or needed some sort of other assistance. Now there was just a swipe machine, a video camera and an intercom. Mostly she just used the swipe machine to get in, occasionally the intercom was required and in honesty she had no idea who or where the owner of the disembodied voice that came over the intercom was. Another technical mystery she thought to herself, although she had a sneaking suspicion that it was just some poor person sat in a windowless room somewhere in the bowels of the building watching the camera and having little interaction with any other human throughout the day.

Once inside she stepped into the elevator and pressed the 4th floor button. 12 years of doing this same commute, 12 years of pressing that same button and 12 years with a lot of the same faces day in, day out. She sighed, in that time her job had morphed through different phases but in reality it had all got a bit too much of the "same shit, different day" feeling about it. She'd been promoted as much as she would have expected and she was rewarded appropriately, in fact she sometimes felt she was likely overpaid for what it was that she did but who's ever going to say that out loud about themselves, really?! She was in the job she had trained for since college and to the outside world she was a great success. And grateful as she was for these things she still felt something was missing. She was bored and craving change and excitement.

Of course it was "change and excitement" which had brought her to this point in the first place. 12 years ago she'd been bored and restless back home in a small town in the south of England and she'd applied for this job in the hope of a grand adventure.

And it had been. A wonderful adventure. Moving to San Francisco and all the things she'd experienced and seen, all the fun she had had in that time, it had created such memories that she never regretted the move ever. But when had she passed that point where she'd become scared to take another leap of faith into the unknown and begin a new adventure?

If only she could… well that was the exact problem, she had no idea what the thing she "could" do to begin another adventure was and whilst she lived her comfortable and safe life where the whole world perceived her as a great success it was hard to take that first step and consider what other options may be available to her.

The elevator doors opened and she stepped out onto the fourth floor. The screen in front of her flashed up the stock price, it was up but not by much and no different from the usual fluctuating; 'I'd better dash to my desk to get that stock price up some more' she thought sarcastically to herself. Presumably that's what the screens were there for, if stock is down folks should rush to their desks to work harder, if stock is up they should rush to their desks to get it up even higher, it was a seemingly never ending grind, feeling like a hamster on a wheel that must keep going but only goes round and round, and it was this she was tired of.

Reaching her desk she was met with the most welcome odor and delightful sight of a plate of bacon, ah lovely Fred! What a glimmer of light he was in her dull, grey day (of course other than the handsome stranger she met earlier today). And even though Fred thought she was crazy for eating it this way he had still left her some ketchup sachets on the side, Heinz ketchup as he is well aware that no other ketchup will do with bacon, what a star he is!

She sat down and docked her phone. The monitor screen came on and the keyboard appeared. The bacon was delicious, she sent Fred a thank you e-card and munched through it whilst scrolling through her newest emails. She was probably one of the few people left who still used email throughout her whole day but her clients were now used to the fact it was far easier and quicker to get a response via email than a call or instant message and she liked to keep it that way, after all lawyers were renowned for being stuffy and stuck in their ways, she could get away with the eccentricity of using such an old fashioned, out of date medium and it suited her to take her time to respond to things rather than being immediately available and always on.

Reading through the message headings, almost all of them marked urgent with that irritating red exclamation point, it was tempting to first deal with the few not marked urgent just for a sense of self satisfaction but all that would breed would be extra "putting this to the top of your inbox" follow up emails, IM pings, text messages and phone calls, she supposed she'd better see what was the most urgent of the urgent group. "URGENT! Contract renewal", sounded thrilling as ever; "URGENT! New celebrity engagement" admittedly this one had the potential to be slightly more thrilling although experience had taught her that celebrity engagements come with a whole host of craziness that you never anticipate and cause endless hours of nonsensical discussions with their team about extra fees they've decided to come up with, mainly, she imagined, just because they could. "URGENT! Do we need a license to use this video", without even opening she suspected the answer was yes. "URGENT! Immediate medical examination required", whoa, what? This was new, she suspected it might be some sort of SPAM or even a virus so she proceeded with caution.

Her eyes scanned the screen to check who the sender was. Interestingly it was coming from the firm of immigration lawyers who represented her company. She felt more confident about being able to open it as it looked like it was coming from a reliable source, although you never can be too careful, email addresses can be cloned, after all. Over the years she'd received all manner of strange requests from them regarding different aspects to the many forms of visa and work permits she had required so she suspected this was just more of the same. She double clicked on the message to read its contents.

Ms Sinclair,

USCIS is requesting that you send them proof that all your immunizations are up to date within 28 working days of this notice.

Proof must take the form of a sealed letter from a doctor listed on the USCIS website as authorized to undertake examinations and immunizations. Please arrange for an appointment with a doctor from this list as soon as possible and send the sealed letter to our address for filing.

Regards

Ed Jones

Paralegal

Ugh, she thought to herself. One of the joys of living in a country of which you are not a citizen is being at the mercy of all their government's requests and feeling you have very few rights or the ability to decline those 'polite' requests. Immunizations! She'd lived there 12 years already and now they were worried about immunizations. Just another scam to feed more money into big pharma no doubt but she supposed she'd better just get on with it and comply with this latest obligation.

She searched the USCIS website for doctors close by and found a practice close to her office that would likely be the easiest place to get an appointment. She gave them a call and explained what she needed, the receptionist who answered her call was obviously very used to these requests. He understood immediately what she needed and was very helpful, this she felt was additional reassurance that this wasn't some sort of scam and it was all very normal practice. As luck would have it they could fit her in at 1pm this afternoon. Might as well take it, she thought, do it and get it over with. With that sorted she turned back to the other urgencies of the morning.

PING! IM from Fred: *So you cheated me out of breakfast, are we set for lunch?*

Reply: *Sure! Have doctor appointment at 1 but we could eat first?*

Fred: *ooh doctor... what's that all about? Food first, leave at 11.30?*

Reply: *11.30 works, tell you over lunch...*

***

At 11.30 promptly Purdy and Fred left through the back door of the building and jumped into Fred's waiting car.

"What shall we have?" Fred asked as he docked his phone

"hmm, I fancy something that's bad for me, I'm grumpy" she replied.

"It's Friday... food that's bad for us is allowed, how about burgers?" she nodded, burgers sounded just what she needed. Fred spoke to the interface: "The Counter, please!" and the car pulled away from the building.

"So... what's the medical emergency? You never go to the doctor, what's hanging off of you to make you go this time? Ooh, ooh I know! You're pregnant! You sly..."

Purdy gently smacked his arm in faux anger "How very dare you?!" they both giggled. "You know how

I love that question, of course that's all women my age do, have babies! No, no it's another visa thing."

Fred looked at her with a confused expression "huh?"

"Oh you know, the government once again wanting more information about me, apparently this time they want to make sure I'm immunized and not spreading my foreigner germs amongst the US citizens."

"Quite right too! You Brits are renowned for your lack of healthcare!" Fred laughed and Purdy smiled at his good natured ribbing, although the NHS was in fact one of the things she missed about living here, she'd never contemplated the cost of healthcare prior to living in this country of sky high medical bills and big pharma drugs that were regularly pushed on patients and she'd learned to appreciate how simple things had been in her home country.

The Counter wasn't too crowded when they arrived, there were a few folks in there, not surprisingly, but they walked in and sat down at a booth. They ordered their burgers and sides from the tablet on their table.

"So, you said you were grumpy. How come? The medical or something else? What can we do to cheer you up?"

"I'm just so bloody bored!", she whined, Fred nodded, this isn't the first time he'd heard Purdy's gripes. "I'm bored with work, I'm fed up with the same old, same old, it gets a little dreary", Fred nodded again, he enjoyed the same old, same old himself. He'd enjoyed a varied career and quite liked what he did right now but he knew from their talks that Purdy was not as settled as him.

"Time to find a new job?"

"Maybe... I don't know, I just don't know what I want. I mean, I have a really nice lifestyle, there are WAY worse situations to be in. I am well aware of how lucky I am it's just, I guess, I'm afraid of change so that's also annoying me too. I miss the days when I was adventurous..."

The robo-waiter sidled up beside them and they took their waters from its tray.

"Maybe you just need a vacation? You always get like this when it's been too long since your last break."

"Maybe," she said, twiddling the paper sleeve from the straw she'd just unsheathed. "vacation doesn't seem like a long enough change though, I'm starting to feel really bogged down. I'm wondering if it's time to move on".

"Well, move on from what? Is it law you don't like anymore? The company? San Francisco? It can't possibly be San Francisco, I won't have it. Not only is it the most fabulous city in the world but I live there too so no reason at all for you to move on from it!"

She smiled "very good point. I think mainly it's a combination of the job and the company. We're lawyers, it sounds way more impressive than what it actually means... lots and lots of paperwork. The problem is, I've been a lawyer for so long it's hard to imagine what on earth I would do instead now."

"Hmm, lets see... what is it that you like doing outside of work that we could turn into a career for you? How about baking? I like your cupcakes, what if you were to bake artisan cupcake batches and deliver them by drone, same day delivery? I'm a genius, what an inspired plan..."

"Undoubtedly a genius but I think baking cupcakes everyday would likely drive me crazy too and, to be fair, I'd end up the size of a house, you know how I love to lick the spoon, that would be a lot of spoons."

"Ugh, how unhygienic! I hope you didn't lick the spoon for the cupcakes you made me last month! I don't blame the government for wanting to check you out for immunizations, you're likely riddled!!!", Fred chuckled to himself, he loved using her British terms on her.

Purdy laughed and threw her napkin at him "so cheeky! I only lick the spoon once the cupcakes are done and in the oven... I promise. I'm also not riddled with anything... except maybe a little fabulousness and I don't know that there is a cure for that."

"Oh so true..." Fred agreed.

The robo-waiter appeared again with their burgers. Both of them had gone for the low carb option of turkey burgers on salad leaves instead of buns but it wasn't all virtuous, Fred ordered a large side of fries and Purdy had ordered fried pickles and a chocolate shake, a veritable feast. They took their plates from the tray and started tucking in.

"Erm, I did not authorize that!" Fred mockingly scolded, nodding towards her chocolate shake and she giggled, choking a little on the gulp she just took.

Many years before, Purdy and Fred had been to see a movie and at the concession stand, whilst Fred was getting popcorn, Purdy had spotted that she could get an ice cream shake on the other side of the counter. She ordered one and as she took her first gulp she heard Fred's voice behind her gasp in mock-shock and say "I did not authorize that!". She had choked then too through a giggle, and because he'd said it so loudly it had caused a ripple of shock on the faces of a young couple stood nearby who thought he was being serious, Purdy knew he wasn't and this made her laugh harder. This was now a standing joke between the pair of them, if Purdy did something Fred was not expecting, he would tell her he did not authorize it and Purdy would giggle, and strangers would inevitably be shocked that this man dared to tell this woman what she could and couldn't do, an intimacy of their friendship that no one else could understand or be a party to, they both enjoyed the exclusiveness of it.

"You know what I regret?" She asked just as she bit into a fried pickle which turned out to be much hotter than she anticipated.

"Biting into that pickle?!" Fred crammed a handful of fries into his mouth, munching happily on the salty potato deliciousness of them.

"Ha, yes that was hotter than I expected! But aside from that I regret not pursuing that helicopter license in the end". Fred nodded as he chewed his mouthful. "I mean, it's not like I could make a second career out of flying helicopters or anything but I did really enjoy it. Remember that week I spent in Florida a few years ago where all I did was fly over the everglades? That was so much fun. I love how when I was flying it was all consuming. My mind didn't wander, there were no distractions, just me concentrating wholly on keeping us in the air. I think the problem with life is there are distractions everywhere, I never get the chance to concentrate on one thing at a time, it's exhausting."

"So, start taking lessons again, what's stopping you?" he took a bite of his burger.

"Nothing, I guess. Although it's been such a long time I'll likely have to start from scratch again. And I'll have to find an instructor here and..."

"And, and... sounds like its something you want to do, I say just do it. Let's google instructors this afternoon, get you up there again, maybe it will help relieve the boredom you're feeling and you'll be less inclined to abandon me to a life of eating fries all alone." He took another handful of fries and looked at his phone, he felt a sense of self satisfaction that he'd fixed all her problems in such a short space of time and now he could concentrate on checking his messages.

Purdy considered the conversation. It was true, maybe Fred was right and that was what she needed. Maybe the daily grind that pretty much everyone she knew experienced was really only bearable when there were extra curricular entertainments that consumed your down time.

"Of course, maybe really all you need is to get laid" Fred continued with a mischievous grin as he looked up from his phone.

"No, no I'm good on that front, thanks, but I appreciate you looking out for me." she responded witheringly, but not before a brief picture of handsome Ben popped into her head, ooh she'd forgotten Ben, maybe she should mention him...

"Changing the subject just a little, are you coming out tonight? I'm meeting some people downtown at 8ish if you want to come too, I think you could do with a night out, it's always fun when you come along."

"Maybe," she replied deciding against mentioning Ben after all "it all depends on how this medical goes, are you guys going VRing?"

"Well of course, what else would we be doing on a Friday night, it's the only way to pass the time!" he was right of course, whiling away the hours with (or even without, to be fair) friends playing in virtual reality worlds was such a great escape.

Of course she had her own VR goggles which she used at home or work for education or entertain-

As she had suspected this was to be a long wait. These days people have become unaccustomed to having to wait for anything. Food arrives quickly, traffic flows smoothly, shopping is delivered within hours of being ordered. There are few places that could continue to operate in today's world where their regular practice was to keep people waiting but that was the joy of medicine, people needed help and had no choice but to wait.

She scrolled through the news app on her phone to distract herself. It was full of the usual predominantly positive stories; Heroic Off-Duty Policeman Saves Young Family From Fire, President Signs New Bill Lowering Taxes (Federal income tax was now only 5% regardless of income, in combination with State income tax which for California was now only 1% for everyone, taxes were vastly improved from just 5 years ago when Purdy was paying up to 50% tax on her income), Crime at Lowest Rate in Recorded History (it was the same story every week, crime rates had been in decline for a decade, this was great and made you feel safe but made for dull reading in reality!).

US Economy Best its EVER BEEN! (hooray, we're all still employable and we can afford to keep our houses, all good, but just as crime rates had been going down, the economy had trended up so this was not new news anymore either), Puppies 'Dance' To Pop Song (aww, she was always a sucker for a cute dog story), Illegal Marijuana Grow Operation Closed Down in Emerald Triangle. To be honest this last one was not necessarily positive in Purdy's opinion, although she understood it would likely be considered a "win" for the general electorate if the most recent elections and law changes surrounding the drug were anything to go by. She knew first hand from seeing how cannabis oil had helped to ease the pain of a dying friend what an unfair reputation marijuana had acquired over the last century.

After moving to California she'd done a lot of research into the subject of weed. She'd found it both surprising and fascinating that it was used so prolifically here when she arrived when in her home country it was so frowned upon. Through her research she found it compelling that the first use discovered was from 3rd Century BC and there is clear evidence that almost every civilization since has used the plant in one form or another for all manner of things and yet there still was no firm evidence of the real long term effects of using the psychoactive part, THC, for medical or recreational use. How could that be? If its been in use that long how can there be no real evidence of the long term effects, other than to those who used as a teenager or whose mother used when pregnant, so really only in those still developing. It made her suspicious and in the days when she'd used social media accounts she'd posted and discussed these things with many others who agreed as well as those who had disagreed. In the end it seems those who disagreed were in the majority and many laws were repealed; both medical and recreational use of cannabis were outlawed once again throughout the United States about five years ago. She had suspicions that Big Pharma were in someway behind it because they would lose too much money if people could grow their own plants to treat their aches and pains, tumors and anxiety amongst other things. When she suggested this again it was a mixed response between people agreeing and those who accused her of paranoia, suggesting she should lay off of using weed that had caused her to become so suspicious. Interestingly, and likely surprisingly, she had never actually been a user of it herself other than one pot brownie a long time ago which had sent her to sleep; although it bored her she held her career in too much high esteem to risk losing her license by using an illegal substance, which her company could test her for at any time, so she'd stuck to the still very much legal vodka, hooray for the demise of prohibition!

She clicked on the dancing puppies video, it was the only thing that was vaguely interesting at this point and she still had time to waste whilst she waited. A litter of 6 black labrador pups appeared on the screen, all in a basket, all bobbing their heads in time to the beat of a pop song she'd heard on the radio in her car recently. Aww, how cute are they, she thought, if only she didn't work such long hours and do such a long commute she'd snap one up in a second. Of course there was always doggy day care, maybe she should look into that, a companion dog might be just the distraction she needed. She loved going for long walks on the beach and at weekends she would get up early to go watch the whales or dolphins at Fort Funston, maybe having a dog to walk might be fun. Really, she wasn't sure she was actually prepared for the responsibility of taking care of another life form but she was 37 now, maybe it was time to become a grown up after all!

"Purdy!" she was suddenly aware of someone calling her name. She looked up and a young woman stood in scrubs and holding a clipboard was peering into the waiting room looking for her.

"Hi, yes, that's me!" she said as she jumped up out of the chair.

"If you'd like to follow me..." Purdy followed her down a corridor and into a side room. It contained a lot of the normal medical equipment you might expect plus what looked like part of a treadmill hooked up to a machine. Oh my, Purdy thought to herself, I hope I'm not going to be expected to run or anything, I'm not sure I can after that shake and fried pickles!

"The doctor will be with you shortly" and with that the woman left the room. Purdy looked around her trying to decide whether to stand or sit. There was the usual examination bed with disposable cover on it, she looked at it. She wasn't sick and doubted she would require laying down at all so it seemed a waste of their cover to sit on that, plus it was high up and her legs would dangle like a six year old at the dinner table. There was a stool with wheels, likely for the doctor, better not sit there. She decided to just lean against the wall, it seemed the best option for now.

After what seemed like forever, but which was more likely 10 minutes the doctor appeared. Purdy only knew she was the doctor because she introduced herself, in reality she looked about 12 years old and surely not old enough to have graduated medical school yet. Purdy began to realize that what she'd been told was true, when policemen start looking like children you know you're now old... apparently the same was true for doctors.

It turned out that this checking for immunizations required a medical examination which included standing on one leg with her eyes closed and touching her toes, although not at the same time. Purdy complied with all the requests, regardless of how ludicrous it felt to her. The doctor enquired into what childhood immunizations she'd had, she reeled off the list she could remember, measles, mumps, rubella, TB, all the usual. She was asked if she had had a recent tetanus shot, she thought she recalled having one three years ago when she fainted and cut her head but she couldn't provide evidence of it right there and then.

The doctor said that she had to take some blood to test for the antibodies of a list of things, including the MMR and, weirdly, syphilis. As Purdy had no evidence of a recent tetanus shot she'd have to have another one, Purdy enquired if it was dangerous to have one if she'd had another recently and the doctor smirked and said no. She didn't know why smirking was required, she thought it was a legitimate question and prudent as she wasn't an expert. She acquiesced and allowed the doctor to give her a tetanus shot. She didn't mind having shots but this one was more painful than she had anticipated and left quite the lump, she was beginning to suspect the doctor was a bit of a sadist or had some weird grudge against her.

She stopped by the reception desk on her way out to pay the bill. $600 for a medical she was being forced into having and which wasn't eligible to be paid for by insurance just seemed like one huge scam!

"Just swipe here." The receptionist pointed her to a laser swipe. Purdy fished around in her pocket to get her phone. She knew this made her look old fashioned and the receptionist gave a perceivable eye roll but, unlike the majority of people these days, she'd refused to have a chip implanted in her hand for making payment. That just seemed one step too far for her, actually having the chip embedded in her person. Like a luddite she stuck with her phone app for payment. She begrudgingly swiped the app to approve the remittance. The receptionist handed her the receipt and still refused to smile or offer any pleasantry.

"Thank you!" Purdy shouted gaily with a big smile as she walked away from the desk. The receptionist firstly looked a little startled then just sneered at her. Lovely, thought Purdy and she opened her app to call for her car. She'd lost the will to do any more work so she decided to just go straight home instead of back to the office. Whilst she waited in the sunshine for her car she messaged Fred to tell him, he inevitably called her a slacker, and said he hoped to see her later. She was still in two minds whether to go out or not but she didn't want to burn any bridges just yet so didn't commit one way or the other. She looked at the car app to see how far away her car was and yawned.

Five minutes later the car pulled up, Purdy jumped in, docked her phone and but her seatbelt on. After the long week she'd had her plan was to sit back and relax in the car on the drive home and read a book that she'd downloaded earlier in the week. It had been recommended by a couple of people to her so she thought it must be worth a read. She opened the book on her phone and projected it onto the dash console. She'd got about 5 pages in and it was showing real promise when she was suddenly interrupted by the interface: MESSAGE RECEIVED, FLO: HEY, YOU FREE TO CHAT? Flo was her old university friend from back home. Instinctively Purdy looked at the clock, it was 2.30pm, 10.30pm on a Friday night in England, she imagined Flo had put the kids to bed, finished her dinner and was settling down with a glass of wine looking for a natter. MESSAGE FLO: SURE, GIVE ME A BELL.

The video screen on the console lit up and started ringing.

"Answer call" she said and started grinning waiting to see Flo's face on the screen. Flo appeared, wine glass in one hand (ah they knew each other so well), waving with the other.

"Hellooooo!" she said

"Hellooooo!" Purdy replied. She loved chatting with Flo, even though she'd lived in the US for many years she still hadn't lost her English accent and tried hard to hold onto her Englishisms. Talking to Flo was one of the few times in the week that she could get through a whole conversation without having to explain what she'd meant by something or repeat it as if she spoke a foreign language. Also Flo was her closest girlfriend even now, even though they were thousands of miles apart they still talked about everything and they were in contact most days.

"How are you? Oh I see you're driving!"

"Yes... well the car is, I was just reading. I'm well thanks, how are you?"

"It's Friday night and I'm having a glass of red after putting the kids to bed so all good here! The car is driving, brilliant, I wish driverless cars had made it to Devon by now! Where you off to?". Unlike California, Britain (along with a lot of places) had been unable to pass the legislation yet for full adoption of autonomous vehicles. They'd done testing but there was still political fighting over concerns around cars being hacked as well as people being reluctant to give up the ability to drive as they actually enjoyed it as a pastime.

"I'm on my way home, just had to have an impromptu trip to the doctor."

"What? Why? You ok?" Flo was suddenly concerned. Purdy explained to her the whole immunization thing and what a pain it was. They laughed about the craziness of it being a requirement after 12 years of her already living there and Flo commiserated with her over the sore lump on her arm following the tetanus.

"So what happens, when do you find out whether you have the right antibodies in your blood or not?"

"The doctor said they'd send the blood to the lab and as long as it all came back ok she'd sign the form for me on Monday. If it comes back and shows I need any further inoculations she'll give me more injections and then sign the form"

"God, what a palaver!" Flo took a sip of her wine and Purdy nodded in agreement. "So what big plans do you have for the weekend? You going out tonight?"

"No big plans, probably just go for a nice long walk at the beach to blow the cobwebs away. Tonight

Fred has invited me out with a group of friends but I haven't decided whether to go or not yet, I might be too tired from loss of blood."

"You wuss! You're fine, go out and enjoy yourself, why not?!" Flo had got used to Purdy's unwillingness to socialize too much and she was concerned that with Purdy being alone all those miles away and cutting herself off from human interactions she could end up really lonely and sad so she was always encouraging her to go out more. She also still held out a small hope that Purdy would find herself a nice man, she knew her friend had little interest and was quite happy staying single but Flo thought it would be nice for Purdy to find someone special.

"I don't know, it's been a long week and what with the car breaking down this morning and the medical this afternoon I'm just a bit over it all to be honest."

"Oh what happened to the car?"

"It turned out to be nothing Ben said it was just..."

"Ben?? Who's Ben?" Flo interrupted her, she hadn't heard of Ben before maybe he was a hottie Purdy was keeping her in the dark about.

"He was the fella who came out with the mechanic vehicle to fix the car"

"Was he cute? As you didn't just refer to him as 'some mechanic bloke' which is the kind of description I'm most used to you using about people I'm suspecting he might be a bit of a hottie??? So what did he look like? What did you chat about? Should I buy a hat?!" Flo was super excited and loved to tease her like this. Besides, Purdy was her only single friend left, everyone else was married with kids and she liked to hear some exciting gossip from over the pond, it was a change in pace from hearing about how little Jemima had weed on the potty for the first time or how Peregrine could sing his alphabet, backwards. Not that she didn't love her friends' children but this was old school entertaining for her.

Purdy sighed, she wished she hadn't mentioned Ben by name and had just called him 'some mechanic bloke' after all, but then again it wouldn't hurt to tell Flo the details and get her thoughts on it although she was cringing a little to herself as the memory over the accusation of him filming her came back to haunt her.

"You've gone red!!! I bloody love video calls, can't hide from me, 'fess up, what does he look like, how are you going to see him again??". Flo poured herself another glass of wine, she was more delighted than ever that she had called her friend now.

"I've gone red because I made of tit of myself and I'm embarrassed reliving the memory so I'm not sure I can actually bring myself to talk about it!"

"No, no, no, no, no! Don't take this away from me, spill, tell me all the embarrassing details. Maybe it wasn't that embarrassing after all, let me judge." She stared at Purdy blinking imploringly at her. Purdy took a deep breath and started to tell her friend the story of her morning.

By the time she finished Flo was laughing at her "Oh my lord, Purd, you're so paranoid!!! Why on earth would he be filming you, you lunatic?!"

"I know, I know, but I saw a weird red light and you know how I am..."

"Yes you're a crazy, paranoid conspiracy theorist but I love you all the same you mad woman!" Flo stopped for a second and it was obvious she was listening out for something. "Oop, I think I hear a child crying... yup definitely hearing that, I'm going to have to dash, call you back really soon, I have thoughts on how we can find this Ben fella again! Much love!!!!" She blew kisses at Purdy as she shut off the call. Purdy waved and blew kisses back and watched the screen until it went black.

They were just slowing as they came up 101 and merging onto Duboce. Wow, nearly home, time flies when you're enjoying a natter. The car stopped at the red light merging onto Market street. She looked out of the window at the street which had once been lined with stores and now was mainly residential housing. Ahead of her, in the spot which once was home to a large Safeway store and an obligatory Starbucks amongst other small stores had been pulled down and replaced by a 6 story block of luxury apartments, housing high tech engineer types from all over the world. She looked up at the balconies, on a couple of them she could see people relaxing, it was a lovely sunny afternoon, it was not late enough for the fog to have rolled in and this area of town was always sunnier than most. An old street car trundled past, along Market Street, painted green, it was full of people, tourists she assumed as it wasn't exactly the most efficient of ways for the locals to get around the city.

The light turned green and the car started to move again. She sat back in the seat and watched out of the window as the car drove along the streets. She lived in a small house on the edge of Buena Vista Park, almost in the absolute middle of the city. Buena Vista Park is high on a hill with views over the city, nestled between the Castro and the Haight districts, sandwiched between the gays and the hippies and she loved it. The car drove on up to the Park, past all the victorian style houses, interspersed with newer, fancier architectural buildings which had been built to replace houses that had become old and tired. She loved them all in their own way. She loved the old style victorians for their character and charm and the newer buildings for their ingenuity. Of all the places she had lived or visited she felt San Francisco was her favorite, so much charm, so much old world meets new, East meets West, antique meets technology, it really felt like the most advanced, integrated and comforting of cities in the world to her.

The car reached the top of Duboce and turned right onto Buena Vista Park East, she reached over and pressed the garage opener button. The car pulled into the garage and docked itself on the charging station. Purdy undocked her phone from the interface and got out of the car, she checked her sky hatch repository for deliveries; groceries and a new pair of shoes. Collecting up her things, she walked through the internal door into her kitchen.

Friday Night Fun

Purdy had been home a couple of hours, had a shower and decompressed somewhat. She'd made the decision she would go join the others for VRing, as Flo said, why not? She deserved to have fun after a long week in the office and at least VRing was a solitary pursuit if she chose it to be, she'd decided she would go and have a go at the helicopter adventure she'd seen advertised. She hadn't tried it before as it was a bit too "real life" for her VRing tastes, she usually liked to try out adventure or historical experiences. Or scary experiences that she really would never try in real life, like white water rafting. But as she and Fred had talked about her taking up her lessons again she thought why not give it a try tonight, remind herself of the basics, see if it was something she'd like to get into again. It was also something she could do solo and she wasn't really in the mood to join a group game tonight.

She made the decision not to tell Fred she was coming, that way she might be able to sneak in and out without having to join in the drinks and food part of it, or if she felt like it she could claim she'd decided to surprise them all and turn up at the last minute. She considered her options of getting there, the easiest was to take the car, she loved the fact that it could park itself and she didn't have to worry about driving round and round the streets looking for parking anymore. She'd never been one to have good parking karma, unlike Fred who seemed to be able to find a spot even if it was a day when there were sports games and concerts going on, he had a gift. She'd been cooped up in the office all week, though so she considered walking. It was about a mile and half to Market and 10th, which was reasonable, and to get there it was mostly downhill or flat. Following the reduction in crime rates she also felt safe walking around the city at most times of the day and night, plus with no drivers and only automated vehicles on the roads, it was only the crazy cyclists that might make an unexpected life threatening decision which she had to look out for when crossing the street.

Of course the walk was not without its perils, at the very top of Duboce, between Buena Vista Park and Castro, the road was extremely steep, a 27.9% grade at its highest point, but affords a fantastic view down to the Bay. She gingerly walked down the hill, glad she'd once again chosen to wear flat sneakers, heels would be impossible on this gradient. Once she got to Castro she realized that it was slightly too warm for all this walking after all, she decided jumping on the Muni was a better plan, at least it was air conditioned down there. The N line no longer ran by Duboce Park unfortunately so her choices were to continue down to Church Station or go down to Market Street towards Castro Station, she picked Castro so she could pop in one of the final convenience stores left in the neighborhood and pick up a packet of gum.

When she reached the station she fished out her phone and opened the payment app. She swiped it at the barrier machine, but nothing happened. She looked at the screen, the funds were there but for some reason it wasn't acknowledging the app. She tried again, again nothing happened. She looked around to see if there were any humans who could help, the booth that used to be manned had long been closed up with no sign of life. She contemplated jumping the barrier but looked around at all the cameras and assumed she would be hunted down immediately; as crime rates were low these days things like fare skipping were treated with more contempt and transportation police had time to follow up regarding such violations.

She looked around, there was an intercom on the wall with a help sign above it, she went over to check if it was in service. She pressed the button.

"Yes?" a voice came through the intercom.

"Er, hi," she replied "the, erm, machine won't acknowledge my app?" she was met with silence. She waited a few seconds. "Hello?"

"Malfunction due to multiple transmissions, payment has been taken from the app, please proceed to barrier 1 for entry".

"Oh, ok thanks" Purdy was surprised at the efficiency and intrigued by the 'multiple transmissions' comment, not really sure what that even meant.

"You're welcome, have a nice day", the intercom clicked off.

She went back to the barriers, barrier 1 opened and she walked through it and took the stairs to the inbound platform, the Muni arrived within moments and she got on.

She came out of Van Ness Station a few minutes later and walked the block to the Augmented Reality Studios. When she entered the building it was already pretty busy, there were people chatting to each other and scrolling through menus to pick the experience they were interested in. She walked up to one of the spare ticket machines and started scrolling through the options. She punched *Helicopter* into the key pad and a list of helicopter experiences popped up.

Escape from Alcatraz was the first title, she read the description but it seemed this involved the player eventually escaping from Alcatraz by grabbing a rope dangling from a helicopter as opposed to being at the controls of one, she scrolled on down the page. *Heli-ski,* jump out of a helicopter and ski down a mountain, *Heli-board* same but on a snowboard, she made a mental note that she would check these out some other time. She quite enjoyed winter sports as experiences and it might be exhilarating to add a helicopter jump into the mix, but not what she was looking for right now. *Fly over the Golden Gate*, this one it seemed was just a sit back and watch experience, this reminded her of the Disney Soarin' ride she once went on in Anaheim, only it was likely this would be a major upgrade in experience due to advancements in technology.

Take Control! was the next title, this seemed more like it. The description stated it was a chance to experience how to take off, fly, hover and land a helicopter. Bingo! Exactly what she was looking for, although she doubted that it would be possible to learn all that in one evening it was a good start and if she enjoyed it she could always come back and keep practicing.

She waved her phone over the screen to activate her VRing account. ACCOUNT NOT RECOGNIZED

TRY AGAIN, the screen flashed an ugly warning sign at her. Weird, there must be something wrong with my phone screen she thought what with this and the muni. She swiped it over again. PLEASE CALL FOR HELP was the message she got this time. She pressed the help button on the machine in front of her. A ringing noise came from it then a voice spoke.

"Hello?"

"Hi, yes, for some reason the machine won't recognize my account, is there someone who can help?" she asked quietly, she was always concerned about drawing attention to herself but in reality absolutely no one was paying any attention to her, they were all caught up in their own activities.

"Miss Sinclair?" the voice asked. Well obviously something was working as they know that much about her at least.

"Yes!" she replied earnestly.

"The machine has recorded a malfunction with your payment app. If you would like to bring your phone to the door to the left of the elevator bank behind the gold pillar, we have a way to troubleshoot the situation". She looked around, she'd never really noticed any doors before, she usually just got straight in the elevator and went to the studios.

"OK, coming" she said and she started to walk towards the elevator bank. She was intrigued, was she going to get to see behind the scenes? For the second time today she was going to have to deal with a stranger but at least this time it seemed it would be a quick fix, they sounded like they knew what was wrong anyway and there was a way to deal with it.

She scuttled past a group of revelers who were laughing about the experience they were planning on playing tonight. She didn't hear the whole description but it sounded like they were going to be playing war games and were trying to decide who was going to be on whose team, apparently the losing side was going to have to buy dinner afterwards so the competitive amongst them were trying to make sure they got the experienced sniper on their side.

The crowd had cleared completely by the time she'd got close to the elevators, one elevator had just left so there was no one waiting and she had a clear view of the room. Past the enormous gold pillars she saw the door to the left of the elevators and walked directly towards it. The door pretty much blended with its surroundings, it was the same shade of cream as the rest of the wall, hence why she had likely never noticed it before. There was no sign on the door indicating what was beyond it, was it a room? A cupboard? She was wondering this as she lifted her hand to knock.

Before she had even made contact with the door it opened rapidly, she jumped in surprise, a huge man in a uniform stood before her. She opened her mouth to speak but before she said anything the man beckoned her into the room.

"Come in, Miss Sinclair." he said abruptly.

She walked in through the door and as the door closed behind her she barely had a chance to take in what the room looked like before the man grabbed her roughly around the torso pinning her arms to her sides with his huge arms and the bulk of his weight. She was so shocked her brain didn't have time to acknowledge what was happening. Without even thinking she began squirming to try and get free from his grasp and opened her mouth to scream when a hand with a handkerchief folded in the palm of it closed over her mouth and nose.

The sickly sweet smell of the chloroform that soaked the material quickly penetrated into her mouth, nose and lungs, as her breathing quickened in panic the icy cold of it consumed her respiratory system. She realized that this was now completely beyond her control, no matter how hard she tried she wasn't go to escape this, she thought she was possibly dying. Her extremities went numb and the last hazy image she saw before passing out were the other uniformed people in the room, two more men and a woman, all looking at her, none of them attempting to help as she struggled. Swiftly, she blacked out.

Confusion

Purdy started to stir. Her whole body ached and her head felt like it was splitting in two. As she struggled to open her eyes she tried to see through the fog in her brain, what had she been doing? She felt hungover but had no immediate recollection of a night out. As the fog cleared it slowly came back to her. The door, the room, the man, the hand, the terror, the black. She forced her eyes to open and squinted against the bright light.

Where was she? She was lying in what appeared to be a single bed with a yellow duvet covering her. The bright light turned out to be bright sunshine which was streaming through a window on the wall where the head of the bed was positioned. She tried to sit up, her head was swimming and she felt a little sick from the dizziness. The room started to come into focus, it was a small room with only space for the bed, a desk and chair which were against the wall opposite the bed and a small closet by a door which was ajar and past which she thought she caught a glimpse of what looked like an en suite bathroom, she could see a toilet at least. Then there was another door which was shut but had no markings on it, no window she could see out of, she presumed that led to the outside world. The walls were painted a similar yellow to the duvet, ugh she thought to herself, she hated yellow, what was with all the yellow?

Hanging on the back of the chair was her handbag. The room was so small she reached across from where she was sat and grabbed it. She looked inside and was relieved to see her phone in there, this was all a little weird, maybe she was in a hospital or something? She pulled her phone out of her bag to see if there were any clues on that as to where she was. The time showed it was 11.07am, gosh she'd really been knocked out... knocked out by what though? And by who? So many questions. There were a couple of messages on the phone. Fred from the night before asking if she was coming out and Flo asking if she'd gone out and if so had she had a good time. She dropped the phone back in her bag. No point in replying to either right now, she needed to work out where she was.

She gingerly got out of the bed and shuffled towards the bathroom. She was wearing an oversized nightshirt that she'd never seen before, maybe it was a hospital gown? It had yellow piping, of course, she thought, yellow must be the corporate color. The bathroom housed a toilet, a small sink and a shower. On the edge of the sink sat a brand new tube of toothpaste and a toothbrush still in it's packet. It was an old school toothbrush like the dentist used to give away, a plastic handle with bristles on the end, not like the sonic brush she had at home.

She checked out her reflection in the mirror over the sink, she looked a little pale and her hair was disheveled but other than that nothing remarkable to report. She recalled the hand across her nose and mouth with the cloth in it and put her hand up to her face, it was tender to her touch and felt a little raw, she was surprised it showed no visual indications of how it felt. Suddenly overwhelmed by a sense of nausea she crouched down and just managed to reach her head over to the toilet in time as she wretched and expelled the contents of her stomach.

She sat there on the bathroom floor leaning against the wall for a while welcoming the cool feeling of the tiles on her skin, still feeling woozy, contemplating the last few memories she could recall. Pushing up the sleeve of her night gown she checked her aching arms. There on her upper arms was the evidence that her memory wasn't failing her completely. Right there were the ugly bluish purple marks of a large hand's fingerprints where the huge man had grabbed her tightly. She was struck with a sense of panic, what had happened to her? And who had found her and brought her here?

Carefully she stood up again, leaning on the sink for support. Her hand turned on the cold tap and she splashed her face with the cooling water, it felt good against her skin and helped to somewhat clear more of the fog from her brain. She took the toothbrush out of the packet and brushed her teeth to get rid of the vile taste in her mouth.

She walked out of the bathroom and looked around for more clues. She went towards the door and turned the handle, it seemed to be locked because she couldn't turn it, she jiggled the handle to see if she could get it to move, it remained rigid. She considered shouting for help but then reconsidered, maybe she just needed to collect herself a bit more, didn't want to look like a mad woman in front of strangers. She went over to the window to see if there were any clues to where she was. Looking out she realized she was obviously not in a San Francisco facility, the view was of rolling hills that went on for miles, other than that there was really nothing to see. It looked like there might be an electricity pylon in the distance, likely a couple of miles away, but other than that it was all trees and fields with no other distinguishing marks.

Puzzled she looked around the room, where were her clothes she wondered. She went over to the closet by the bathroom door and opened it. No sign of her clothes in there but there were 3 yellow t-shirts folded up on a shelf, 3 pairs of yellow trousers hanging from coat hangers and 3 sweaters, yes also in yellow, hanging there too. Neatly folded on another shelf were 3 pairs of underwear, in a fetching shade of nude and 3 bras, also in nude. Three of everything, maybe they were all different sizes? Small, medium and large, something for anyone who finds themselves here without their clothes? She checked for labels, but there weren't any. This was all so weird, the sense of panic was getting more and more fierce and she could feel her heart racing. Suddenly a searing pain shot through her forehead and she stumbled backwards and plonked down on the bed. It was throbbing, she laid down and closed her eyes.

She must have fallen back to sleep, she woke again feeling groggy and still confused. She was still in yellow hell, still none the wiser about where she was. On the desk now was a bottle of Smart Water (no regular bottled water here, you got electrolytes with your mystery stay) and a sandwich. She reached over and picked up the bottle, undoing the seal she took a few slugs, it felt fantastic as the cool water hit her throat and she felt it flow down her esophagus. It also almost felt like it was directly re-hydrating her brain as it helped breakthrough the mist and ache in her forehead. She looked at the sandwich, she still felt queasy and decided against it, besides it felt odd that she had no idea where it had appeared from and it seemed foolish to eat something with no knowledge of its origin.

She sat up and drank some more. Feeling a little better she got up off the bed and tried the door handle again, still no movement. She knocked on the door with her fist "HELLO?!" she shouted and then listened. No response. "HELLO!! Is anyone out there?". Nothing. Lacking the strength to do much more she sat back down on the bed.

She remembered her phone and rummaged in her bag for it. Pulling it out she noticed it was now 12.23 so she had seemingly fallen back to sleep for about an hour. She unlocked the phone and contemplated who to contact. Maybe she should call someone and tell them where she was, or at least tell them she appeared to be locked in a room but she didn't know where she actually was. She decided to try Fred. She dialed his number "call cannot be con-nected at this time" said the message in her ear. Next she tried Flo, same message again. The panic was starting to rise in her again so this time she just tried a random client's number just to see if it would work, same message again. OK, she thought to herself, this might be over the top but I'm trying it anyway. She dialed 911. It fast ran through her brain that she didn't know what she would say but she was pretty sure they had the ability to track where her phone was if she explained she was confused and appeared locked in a room, surely they'd have to help her. The unwelcome message played in her ear again, "call cannot be connected at this time". Shit!

OK, new plan, maybe a text… MESSAGE FRED: URGENT! CAN YOU CALL ME? She waited for what seemed like an age for a response nothing came so she followed up with another.

MESSAGE FRED: OK I KNOW THIS WILL SOUND ODD BUT CAN YOU PLEASE TRY TO CALL ME? OR AT LEAST SEND ME A TEXT? SOMETHING WEIRD HAPPENED TO ME LAST NIGHT, I THINK I MIGHT HAVE BEEN KIDNAPPED. LONG STORY BUT I'VE WOKEN UP IN THIS LOCKED ROOM WHERE EVERYTHING IS BLOODY YELLOW BUT NO OTHER CLUES AS TO WHERE I AM AND I CAN'T FIND ANYONE TO HELP ME

No response. Shit, shit.

MESSAGE FLO: CAN YOU TALK? She twiddled the phone in her fingers whilst she waited for any reply. She could see all messages had been delivered but sadly it seemed neither of them had noticed her messages yet.

She stared down at her phone and considered other options. Maybe the internet? Even if she didn't use them as a matter of course she still could get access to her social media accounts, maybe she could try and get a message to someone that way?

Her thoughts were interrupted by the appearance of a projected monitor on the wall ahead of her. She jumped, as a woman's face appeared on the screen.

"Hello Miss Sinclair and how are you feeling?"

"What? What the…? Where am I?!" she mustered.

"Please don't worry, Miss Sinclair, you're completely safe," Purdy stared at the image, so many questions swirling around her head, so much confusion. "I know you must have many questions," the woman continued in a strangely soothing voice "and I can answer them all, I'm here to help you, are you ok? Are you not hungry? We sent your favorite sandwich."

"My favorite…? What…?" she trailed off and looked at the untouched sandwich. It was actually debatable that she had a favorite sandwich in reality, it depended on her mood and in what country she was in she had found. In England she liked ham and tomato with a slick of mayonnaise, preferably on a soft white bap. In California she usually opted for turkey, brie and cranberry on sourdough. She realized she was looking at a sourdough sandwich and caught sight of what seemed to be turkey, brie and cranberry. "How...?"

"You must be wondering where you are" the woman had a kind looking face, somewhat motherly, it put Purdy a little at ease but she was still freaked out by the whole situation, she nodded her head. "Don't worry, you are perfectly safe, we are here to look after you. Do you remember how you got here?"

"I remember being attacked..." Purdy began.

"Attacked?" the woman looked concerned "Who attacked you?"

"I was in the Augmented Reality Studios, my app wasn't working, I was told to go to a door for help and the man behind the door grabbed me, that's all I remember."

"Oh you poor dear, you seem to be suffering from hallucinations. You were brought here by ambulance when you collapsed during your VRing experience." Purdy contemplated this, surely that's not true, she distinctly remembered the door, the man, and the hand. "You were weak from giving blood earlier in the day and you got hot in the studio, you hit your head when you fell and became unconscious, you were brought here as a precaution. Maybe the attack was part of your VRing experience and you are just confusing the memory?"

"But I..." Purdy was so confused, none of this made sense, she never made it to the studio and besides she'd picked a helicopter flight, not one of the escape games. She lifted the sleeve of the night gown to show the woman the bruises. "Look, I have bruises from where I was grabbed, that wouldn't happen from an VRing experience."

The woman smiled "Those are just from where you fell over and people tried to help you."

Purdy was not convinced "I don't understand any of this. How do you know about me giving blood? And by the way, why is the door locked? Where the hell am I? Why can't I make phone calls? I feel like a bloody prisoner."

"Please calm down, Miss Sinclair, it is not good for you to get upset."

"You need to answer my questions otherwise I'm going to get really bloody upset and I'm going to start complaining very loudly."

"All your questions will be answered, of course. First off, you are at a medical facility. You were brought here due to your health issue. We know about you giving blood because we have a copy of your medical records which we had to get a copy of in order to provide you with the correct care." Ok, at least this seemed to make sense to Purdy. "The reason the door is locked is because, due to the tests that were run on your blood we have had to quarantine you for a short time."

Quarantine? What the? "What's wrong with me???" Purdy was frantic, this was all too much, she only went for the medical as a matter of course, she never felt unwell, how could she need to be quarantined?

"Please do try not to worry, Miss Sinclair, it is merely a precaution until we know for sure that you are not contagious."

"What have I got?" it was hard for Purdy to care about whether she was contagious or not when she didn't know the severity of whatever it was she supposedly had herself.

"The tests found evidence of the tuberculosis virus in your blood, you have to be quarantined for a statutory period of 5 days while we carry out further tests. Tuberculosis is an incredibly contagious disease and we are required to do this by law."

TB? Really? But she had been inoculated against this as a child, none of this made any sense but what could she do?

"So I have to stay here, in this room for 5 days all alone?"

"Yes, but we will provide you with entertainment and sustenance for all that time and will try to keep you as comfortable as is possible. Think of it like a mini-vacation!"

This is not where I would choose to vacation, she thought to herself.

"But what about work?"

"We have informed your employer, don't worry about a thing." sure it was great her keep saying not to worry but Purdy had responsibilities. "As for making phone calls I'm afraid that sometimes the reception is spotty in here, keep trying and you'll get it to work eventually. If you need to charge your phone please just place it on the desk, it is fully enabled to wirelessly charge devices. Also, please feel free to use the shower and change into the clothes in the closet. It might help make you feel better and they should all be the correct size. We provided you with a toothpaste and toothbrush and some toiletries that you may require to make your stay with us more comfortable."

"You don't happen to have anything but the yellow clothes do you? Not a big fan of yellow." Purdy knew this was the most ludicrous of things to say when there were still so many unanswered questions but it just came out. The woman just smiled at her and then disappeared from the screen.

"Hello?" Purdy called out, no response "Hello? How do I call you if I need you?" Her question was met with silence.

Five Days?!

Five days? I have to spend five days locked in this tiny yellow hell? Purdy was in shock. None of this seemed to make any sense and she was struggling to think straight. She looked at her phone to see if anyone had replied yet, nothing. She looked out of the window again, at least the view was quite tranquil, she thought, but being able to see the ocean would have been more relaxing. She wondered how close to the ocean she was and it occurred to her she could check the map app on her phone. She opened it up, usually the location would appear in nanoseconds, but she was left looking at the whirring circle of the past, they really do struggle with connectivity here she thought, it's like in the days of 4G and LTE. She watched the circle whir and whir but eventually it just stopped, unable to connect at this time. She put the phone on the desk to charge it up and felt despondent.

Maybe things would look a little clearer if she were to take a shower as the woman had suggested, if nothing else it might help with her aches and pains and make her feel more awake. She went into the bathroom and turned on the shower, she was pleasantly surprised that the stream of water flowed hard and fast and was the perfect temperature. She took off the night gown, it dropped to the floor and she stepped into the hot shower stream. The soothing water cascaded down her aching body, she slowly turned around to allow it to flow over all of her aching muscles. She looked down at her poor arms. Bruised from her fall (she still wasn't sure she believed this but it was possible that her memory had played tricks on her of course) and covered in needle marks from the blood she'd had taken and the immunizations she'd been given, she looked like some sort of heroin addict, what a mess. There was still a lump on the upper portion of her left arm from the tetanus shot that she ran her hand over.

It was possibly one of the longest showers she'd ever taken, the water temperature and pressure remained constant and she just stood there indulging in it. On the shelf in the shower was shower gel, shampoo and conditioner. All brands that she had tried at some point but didn't use often as they were expensive and smelt divine. When she got out she wrapped herself in the huge fluffy yellow towel that hung on the back of the door and wrapped her hair in the smaller yellow towel by the sink. She realized the mirror above the sink was in fact the door of a thin cabinet and she opened it to find moisturizer and q-tips amongst other things, she used everything she would have at home. She looked in the mirror again, now scrubbed clean and feeling fresh she looked her normal self, other than being surrounded by yellow fabric and feeling slightly bruised.

She walked back into the bedroom to find that the sandwich had gone but another bottle of water had been left on the desk along with a can of Diet Dr Pepper and a bag of salt and vinegar chips. She felt uncomfortable with the fact that someone had obviously been in there whilst she was in the shower and she tried the door handle again, it was still locked. She sat on the edge of the bed and the monitor screen appeared again, the woman was smiling at her. Purdy felt exposed and pulled the towel around her more tightly, in normal circumstances she would have chastised the woman over her lack of concern for Purdy's privacy but as she needed answers she didn't want to piss the woman off.

"Hello Miss Sinclair, I hope you enjoyed your shower. How are you feeling?"

"I'm ok, thanks" she realized the nausea had now passed and had been replaced with hunger. Her headache had somewhat lifted and she actually was feeling a little better.

"Good, good, we had some chips delivered and some more drinks, if you have any requests for dinner please do let me know, we want you to feel comfortable"

"Well as you mention it... I find it a little uncomfortable that it seems someone is entering the room when I am asleep or in the shower and you just pop up out of nowhere but I have no way of contacting you when I need something." Purdy watched for the woman's reaction but she barely raised an eyebrow.

"Of course, that must be disconcerting" she replied "Don't worry, no one has entered your room, all deliveries are made by drone due to your isolation. If you need anything and would like to talk to someone please press the green button on the side of the desk and someone will contact you as soon as is possible. If you do not wish to be disturbed please press the red button which will let us know that you wish for privacy."

Purdy looked at the side of the desk and wondered why she hadn't noticed the two buttons before. They were right there, although they had no labels on them so it's not like she would have known what they were for if she had found them. And they were quite discreet, flat against the wood of the table.

"So, any dinner requests? Also any entertainment requests? We have access to a broad range of movies and TV shows if you are interested in streaming something to watch or we can loan you an ebook for your phone if you want to read? Of course if you would like time to think about it please do and you can press the green button to let us know what you would like when you decide."

"Do I have internet access at all? Can I make video calls? I really want to tell my friends where I am… actually where am I?!"

"Your phone should be able to get a connection eventually, we have no other way to assist you in connecting to the internet. We suggest that you use messages as these seem to work best. As I mentioned earlier, you are in a medical facility, in quarantine."

"Yes, I got that, I just wondered where, geographically I am, I see the view from the window is all fields, I don't recognize where I am" and by the way, she thought to herself, what kind of modern facility has such difficulty with internet connectivity? She rarely, if ever had connectivity issues in this day and age. What a dive this must be!

"The facility is just outside of San Francisco, not far from where you were VRing."

Hmm, she wasn't sure what 'not far from' meant, she'd collapsed downtown and just outside the city would literally be in the bay from where she was.

"Am I in the East Bay, Oakland maybe?" she asked, it seemed unlikely, she wasn't sure that there was such scenery in Oakland but then again she hadn't spent a lot of time there so it was possible.

"You are in the East Bay, yes"

Purdy wasn't convinced that that was exactly answering her questions fully but decided for now she wouldn't worry about it and she'd just work on trying to get her phone to connect, it would be more helpful than this woman, anyway.

"Oh ok. You know what I really feel like eating? Pancakes, is that possible?"

"Absolutely, would you like them with bananas and chocolate chips? Maybe some bacon on the side too?" Purdy was surprised, this was exactly the way she liked to have pancakes at her favorite brunch spot in the city.

"Er, yes that would be great, thanks. And I think I'd like to watch a movie... do you have Shawshank Redemption?" she thought she could empathize with Andy and Red as she felt a bit of a prisoner herself, although she doubted she would ever need to crawl through 'five hundred yards of shit smelling foulness' to escape from here... at least she hoped she wouldn't.

"Yes of course" and with that the woman disappeared and in her place appeared a movie screen where the film started to play.

Purdy leant over and pressed the red button, she may not have a lot of control over her current predicament but at least she could control the random appearances of this stranger into her temporary boudoir. She then got up and opened the closet, took out one of everything and got dressed. It all fit perfectly, how bizarre, she thought, even when you buy clothes on line there's a margin for error, she comes in here and the first set of clothes she picks up fits her like it was made for her. Well made for her in size, not in color, she looked at her reflection in the bathroom mirror, yup yellow was not her color at all.

After hanging the towels back on the hooks she had taken them from she went back into the bedroom and opened her handbag. Luckily she carried a hairbrush so she could detangle the wet mess her hair had become. She opened the bag of chips and the can of Dr Pepper and sat on the bed to watch the movie. Reaching over to check if she had any messages on her phone yet, and seeing nothing she decided to try messaging Fred again. MESSAGE FRED: I MIGHT NOT HAVE BEEN KIDNAPPED AFTER ALL (ALTHOUGH HOLD THAT

THOUGHT AS THIS IS ALL STILL PRETTY STRANGE) APPARENTLY I AM IN QUARANTINE AS I HAVE TB!! I CAN'T BELIEVE IT. I'LL BE HERE 5 DAYS, NO WORK FOR ME, I'M TOLD TO TREAT IT LIKE A MINI VACATION, I CAN THINK OF BETTER PLACES TO GO! She pressed send and watched the message go, the 'delivered' message popped up and she waited briefly hoping that she'd get a response. Still nothing. She picked up the hairbrush and set about getting her locks under control.

By the time Andy was spending his first night in Shawshank Purdy's pancakes were arriving. She noticed a knock at the door "hello?" she said inquisitively. The top third of the door opened inwards like a cat flap and stayed open. In flew a drone, a tray suspended beneath it. On the tray were the pancakes and they looked and smelt delicious. There was also a chocolate milkshake, she hadn't asked for that but she wasn't about to turn it down either, quarantine was beginning to look less like a punishment that she had first thought, she wished Fred was there to tell her that he hadn't authorized the shake though, it was going to be a lonely pretend vacation at this rate.

It could be worse...

It turned out that the food in the yellow room was delicious and anything she craved was provided. She tested this out after a couple of days by asking for things like dishes from her favorite Thai and Indian restaurants which were "chef's specials" just to see if she really could order anything, and they were delivered, by drone, perfectly cooked and in perfect portion sizes, it really was quite remarkable. Also, she really did have as much entertainment as she required in the form of movies, TV, books and games. She'd even managed to (kind of) make friends with the woman on the screen who she could summon with the touch of the green button. It turned out her name was Priscilla and if Purdy asked her she was quite happy to oblige and play board games or discuss the movie Purdy had been watching. They didn't talk about anything "real", they weren't really friends after all but they could have a pleasant exchange about the game or the show. Priscilla was still not particularly forthcoming with details that Purdy enquired about but her desire to ask waned quickly so this didn't post too much of a problem.

She was getting some of the best rest that she had had in absolutely years too. It was an extremely peaceful place, with no noise outside of her four walls. She heard no other people, no street noise; living in the city she was used to construction or fire trucks and ambulance noise any time day or night, here it was silent. She found that eerie to begin with but it really helped her fall into some deep slumbers when night fall came so she came to appreciate it. Priscilla had been right, she could treat this like a vacation. Of course the down side was that she couldn't leave the room so there was a definite danger of cabin fever setting in and she really felt like she would like to go for a walk in the fresh air but she knew it was only for five days so she thought she may as well make use of the peace and quiet while it lasted. When she had complained to Priscilla that she would like to go for a walk she had been shown that there was a treadmill built into the floor by the window so she could get some exercise if she desired and look at the view from the window as she trained, she'd kept herself busy for about a couple of hours throughout the day on the machine, it helped stave off the cabin fever and also helped her sleep a lot more deeply.

Her phone continued to have spotty coverage. She had managed to receive a couple of messages from Fred who'd sent her his best wishes, said he'd been designated to cover her workload in her absence and teasingly called her a slacker but that was all. She thought it odd that he didn't seem more concerned for her after her initial "kidnapped" messages but maybe he was busy and he'd just put that down to slight hysteria on her part.

Flo had sent messages too, saying she hoped she felt ok and that they could chat when Purdy was back home again. What she didn't miss was email and being always "on", it didn't take her long to get used to not being at anyone's beck and call, her clients couldn't contact her here, no emails, no messages, that was really blissful and this aspect was better than any vacation she'd taken in the last few years because it almost always happened that someone would want or need her when she was away. She surprised herself, though, when she realized that she missed human contact too, for someone who would do anything to avoid other people under normal circumstances she wouldn't have expected to miss people's physical proximity quite so much.

She was having such a lovely time that she seemed to quickly forget the horror and panic she had felt on waking up and not recalling how she got here. In just a four day stay she'd managed to relax and her body had begun to heal so well that she barely remembered the fuzzy memory of the man grabbing her behind the door. She had filed it away in the recesses of her brain and taken what Priscilla had told her as the most likely truth, her memory had played tricks on her back then and she'd merely collapsed during her VRing experience. There were no longer bruises on her arms, the nausea had passed after that first day and she felt better than she had felt in she didn't know how long with all the rest she'd been getting.

With only one night left here she started to dread the thought of going back to work, going back to the stress of it all. Funny, she thought, if only everyone could experience a spot of quarantine, it had really left her feeling wonderful. Getting some fresh air was going to be nice, though.

She was lying on the bed reading a book when she caught sight of the red light blinking out of the corner of her eye. She had come to learn that although when she pressed the red button she got privacy, if Priscilla needed to contact her then she could alert Purdy by flashing the button to get her attention. Purdy pressed the green button to allow Priscilla to appear.

"Hi Priscilla, what's up?" she said brightly.

"You look well, Miss Sinclair!" Priscilla replied, Purdy had tried to get Priscilla to call her Purdy a couple of times but apparently her requests had fallen on deaf ears.

"Well thank you, I feel pretty good too, this has all been very relaxing, I've really enjoyed my time here. Looking forward having a walk in the fresh air tomorrow but no complaints about my stay!"

"Good, we are glad you have enjoyed it. In which case it is my pleasure to tell you that we require that your stay continues for a while longer." Priscilla smiled at Purdy.

"Stay longer?"

"Yes, for a while. The tests we conducted have concluded that you require more time excluded from the general population." Purdy stared at Priscilla whilst she took in this information. "The good news is that you don't have to remain locked in isolation. You will be allowed out of your room and you can mingle with the other inhabitants of this facility!"

Purdy sat there and contemplated this news. An unexpected sense of relief came over her. She considered what she was missing out on by being kept here a while longer. She considered her job, how long would she be here now? She felt unfazed by the fact that she might lose her job if she stayed too long. That in itself was odd, she'd always held her job in such high esteem and it had somewhat defined who she was for the last 15 years.

She thought about her friends, maybe outside of this room her connectivity would be better and she could resume her normal video chat relationship with Flo. She could still keep messaging with Fred. That was really all she needed from them, just occasional contact. Also odd, her friends meant the world to her. Since she lost her parents at a young age she relied on the friendships in her life as a family support network and here she was, after just 4 days, forgetting that strong bond, letting go of that network with such ease.

She did wonder who the other inhabitants were. Were they all being isolated from the general population like her? All of them with diseases? All with TB? Weirdly though she wasn't at all concerned that she might be surrounded by diseased people that may be contagious. She just wondered if they would be friendly to her.

She considered how nice it would be to continue on with this stress free lifestyle. Someone else cooking and cleaning for her, no job to rush to, and now she'd also be able to walk around outside, it might be good to prolong this enforced vacation in reality.

"You will soon be shown to your new room, you no longer need to stay in the medical isolation wing of the facility anymore, you'll be moved elsewhere." Priscilla continued on. "You will be provided with new clothes, I know this will please you, no more yellow!"

"Excellent" replied Purdy, truly uncaring of the fact that her enforced imprisonment was to continue and it never crossed her mind to ask for a second opinion or to speak to anyone else, she had become easily accepting of this state of helplessness. It was like being a child again with someone else worrying about the adult issues, she couldn't think of any reason to make a fuss, she was just too relaxed, let Priscilla do the worrying, Purdy was just going to enjoy living without concerns.

"I hope you enjoy the rest of your stay, Miss Sinclair" Priscilla disappeared from the screen.

Well ok, Purdy thought to herself. She contemplated what new clothes she was going to be provided with, hooray for no more yellow, she really had not enjoyed being surrounded by that color for the last few days. She lay back down on the bed and continued reading her book.

A while later there was a knock at the door and it opened for the first time since her stay began. In rolled a robot akin to a robo-waiter. Past the robot Purdy could see into the corridor outside her room. There was nothing remarkable about it but she did notice that it was painted white, not yellow, which was a welcome change. There were also other doors along the corridor, all closed, she presumed they all housed someone like her, someone who required quarantine. She picked up her bag and followed the robot out of the door. There was no need to take anything else with her, she'd only come in with her handbag after all, everything else had been provided for her.

The corridor was well lit, there was no outside light at all and none of the doors had windows, just like her door hadn't. It was quiet and no noise came from anywhere. She followed the robot down the hallway until they reached an elevator. They got into it but there were no buttons to press, the elevator just closed the doors and descended to the ground floor.

The door opened, she felt a cool fresh breeze on her face and it felt so good, really refreshing. The elevator had opened onto what looked like a parking lot. She took her first steps outside in four days and looked around but it was dark with only the glow from a very slight moon shedding light on her surroundings. It was hard to make out what she was looking at, and she wondered how far it was to her new lodgings.

A car pulled up and the door opened, the robot spoke for the first time telling her to please get into the car and she would be taken to another part of the facility. She happily got into the car wondering what she might see on the way. She closed the door and it locked, it was pitch black outside and the car used no headlights. Automated cars didn't require headlights like manual cars did, it wasn't like they needed to "see" like human drivers needed to, they were aware of their surroundings using GPS signals and other sensors. You were required to use them on the public roads in order to be seen but if this was a private facility there was no legal requirement for headlights, and presumably no facility requirement.

They drove through the dark at about 20 miles an hour for about 10 minutes. Purdy squinted out of the windows during the drive to see where she was. It was a dark night, with little moonlight to light the way, the lights inside the car were on so she could see little else but her own reflection staring back at her. The car appeared to turn a corner and in the distance she could see what looked like the outline of a building with a few dotted windows lit up. The car drove towards it, this seemed to be their destination.

The car stopped and another robot was there to greet her. The car door swung open and she picked up her bag and got out. The robot wheeled away and she followed in its wake, presuming that that was what was required of her, walking quickly to keep up. They walked directly towards the building she'd been watching in the distance.

The door to the building opened as they approached, Purdy followed the robot inside and they turned right down another white corridor lined with more windowless doors. One of the doors was open, the robot went inside and Purdy followed. She chuckled to herself, the room was almost identical to the room she had just left only it was decorated in pale blue instead of yellow, Purdy felt a sense of relief, she found blue a much more calming color to live with.

The robot left the room and closed the door behind it. Purdy looked around, it really was pretty identical, she opened the closet and as she had suspected it housed three identical outfits once again, only this time in blue instead of yellow. Funny place, she thought to herself, maybe they color coded the people so they didn't lose track of them, or maybe it just made laundry easier.

She found the green and red buttons on the desk just like the yellow room. She requested to have a TV show played and pressed the red button to ensure she wasn't disturbed, then got into bed and fell into a deep sleep.

Out of isolation

Purdy was awoken from her deep sleep by a knock on the door. She opened her eyes and noticed that it was already light outside. She heard the knock again, she wasn't used to two knocks, the drones and the robot had just knocked once then entered.

"Hello?" she called out

"Hello!" came a woman's voice "Can I come in?"

"Erm, sure" she was still wearing her yellow clothes from the day before so it didn't feel too weird to invite her stranger into her bedroom as she lay in bed but she sat up to receive her impromptu guest.

The door opened and in walked a middle aged woman dressed in an identical outfit to her yellow one, only in the pale blue hue that was in Purdy's new closet.

"Hi! I'm Jenny, welcome to the Blue Mansion!" Jenny was a little too perky for this time of the morning.

"Hi, my name's Purdy, pleased to meet you." Blue Mansion? She thought to herself as she wrapped the duvet around after her feeling slightly vulnerable sitting in bed with a complete stranger at her door.

"I'm going to grab breakfast, I thought you might like to join me?" Purdy considered the invite, she realized this was her first chance to interact with other human beings in five days and even though it went against every fiber of her being to make new friends in general it would likely be a good thing to talk to someone else while she was here. She was also intrigued and had questions about her fellow inhabitants and maybe Jenny might have more answers than Priscilla ever came up with.

"Oh yes, that would be great, do I have time to get dressed first?" Purdy looked down at her yellow outfit that was crumpled from sleep.

"Totally! How about I come back in 20 minutes? Give you time to wake up a bit?"

"Thank you, I really appreciate that!" Jenny nodded in acknowledgment and closed the door as she walked out.

Purdy stretched and got out of bed. Time for a quick shower she thought to herself. She went into the bathroom and was greeted by the same sight as the yellow bathroom, only in blue. It also had the same products. She stripped off the yellow clothes for the last time feeling a little gleeful and jumped in the shower contemplating the conversation she might have with Jenny.

Right on cue 20 minutes later there was another knock at Purdy's door, she went over to open it, happy to once again not feel locked in, the door opened as she put her hand on the knob, Jenny's face appeared in the gap.

"Hi again! Ready now?" Still perky. She was likely to become annoying and Purdy was slightly irritated at the fact that she just opened the door to let herself in but she wasn't about to make a big deal of it as she had questions to ask so she just smiled.

"Yup, I'm ready, let's go!" it reminded her somewhat of her first day at university when she moved into her halls of residence. That time it had been Flo who knocked on her door to see if she wanted to go for a pint. She was lucky that Flo was so outgoing and approached her otherwise she may have had a quite lonely time at university. Maybe Jenny would be her savior here in... well that was one of the questions wasn't it, where? Where were they?

Purdy grabbed her phone from the desktop and stepped out into the corridor in her new blue outfit, shoving the phone into her pocket. There was no one else in view, just her and Jenny. Surely there must be more people here, she thought to herself, and wondered how far they were going to go for breakfast. Not that she minded, she was looking forward to getting outside in the fresh air today.

"So, how do you like your room?" Jenny asked brightly. Odd question, Purdy thought, but maybe Jenny was just trying some small talk to get the conversation started.

"Oh it's nice, thanks. I mean, identical to the last one I was in but I do prefer the blue color to that yellow they had in the other one!" she knew this was pointless drivel but she wasn't good at small talk either.

Jenny smiled "oh I remember the isolation yellow, it's one of those colors that you love or hate, eh?"

"Yes! It's certainly not my favorite and that was a lot of yellow to take in one go!" she smiled, it was nice to have a chat like this after 5 days on her own, Jenny seemed easy going.

They got to the end of the corridor and as the door to their left opened the bright sunshine flooded the entrance way. They walked out into the daylight and Purdy gasped, she was not expecting the view she was faced with. It was like walking onto the set of a movie.

Directly in front of them was a large square of perfectly manicured grass. In the middle of it was a huge, beautiful fountain with sparkling blue water cascading out of it into the deep pool below.

Beyond the grass and straight across from where they were stood a large ornate white building, with pillars and elaborate arches. It reminded her of somewhere she had once been but she couldn't put her finger on where. She stood wondering and it occurred to her that it was built in colonial style, much like Raffles Hotel in Singapore where she'd once stayed when she travelled in Asia. She had pushed the boat out once arriving in Singapore after having roughed it through several other Asian countries and she'd wanted to visit Raffles ever since watching Tenko with her mum as a child, where the ladies locked up in the prisoner of war camp reminisced about Singapore Slings in the grand hotel.

The building had three distinct signs equally spaced across the front of the building; the first read Cafe, the middle one simply said Gym and the final one said Art. To their left was a large building also painted in white, and to the right was an identical sized building painted in red. Purdy turned to look at the building they had walked out of. Once again it was an identical size, only this building was pale blue. She wondered if the identical white, red and blue buildings were all the same, all housing rooms like the one she was staying in.

A paved, circular road surrounded the square of grass and four other roads linked to the circular disappeared off between the four buildings, one at each corner of the larger square that the buildings made. It was all very well kept, the lawn perfectly manicured, no trash, no dirt, everything spotless and symmetrical. There were no cars or trucks anywhere to be seen, not even a bicycle, it seemed everyone here must walk. There were cobbled paths running across the grass all meeting at the centerpiece fountain.

Dotted all over the place were people, all dressed in the same outfit as Purdy and Jenny, mostly pale blue but interspersed with some people dressed in black. Purdy stood there a little flabbergasted, she wasn't sure what to make of where she was, this was the "facility" that Priscilla had told her she was staying in - but what sort of a facility? She had imagined it would be like a hospital but this appeared to be like a perfectly manicured town square. On the one hand it was eerie with the immaculateness of it all and the identically dressed people and on the other it was quite breathtaking.

"Where the heck are we?!" Purdy enquired of Jenny.

"It's pretty amazing, isn't it?" Jenny beamed at Purdy. "C'mon!" she said as she walked towards the path closest to them that led to the fountain.

Purdy followed behind her looking around in bemusement, this was not at all what she had expected to see outside those doors. They passed by a group of people sitting playing chess with one another. Some of them looked up from their games and smiled and nodded, others continued staring at their boards in concentration, apparently contemplating their next moves. Jenny said hi to a couple of women who were walking towards them, they smiled and said hi to Purdy. She was unused to such interactions and managed an awkward smile and nod back then looked away quickly.

As they made their way towards the fountain the tremendous sound of the falling water filled their ears. It was such an awesome sound, the water cascading and crashing into the pool below, Purdy stopped and took it all in. She thought she could stand there for hours and just watch it, the water constantly changing and falling with the sunlight dancing off of it and making rainbow patterns. Jenny tugged at her sleeve, apparently she'd been urging Purdy to come along but Purdy hadn't quite heard her with the distraction of watching the fountain and the noise of the water crashing. Disappointed at the interruption but still intrigued to see more she quickly started following Jenny again past the fountain and down the path that led in the direction of the doorway marked Cafe.

""I hope you're hungry!" Jenny said as they reached the door "So many lovely options to choose from, my favorite is the french toast, but I try to limit myself to only eating that at weekends..." her voice trailed off as she entered the door. Purdy following behind was hit by the deliciously welcoming smell of freshly cooked bacon and realized she was actually quite peckish and looking forward to seeing what they had on offer in this Cafe.

First impressions

The inside of the Cafe was well lit and extremely clean and tidy. The room was filled with tables, all with room for 4 people to sit at each of them. Some were full with people eating and chatting away, others were free and welcoming. There were robo-waiters dotted about the place, some were wiping tables, some were delivering food or taking it away and some were just docked by the wall, presumably waiting to spring into action.

Purdy followed Jenny to a table at the edge of the room by a window which overlooked the grass lawn and fountain. As they walked past the other diners Jenny said hi to some of them, everyone replied in kind and smiled past her to welcome Purdy. So unlike the world she was used to Purdy further felt awkward and only smiled briefly before looking away. This place might be too friendly for her comfort levels. Jenny sat down at the table and Purdy took a seat on the opposite side facing her. There was a tablet at the edge of the table which displayed the menu, and from which they were to order.

"Oh, no prices, hope that doesn't mean this place is super expensive!" Purdy said without really thinking, it wasn't like she couldn't afford it but she was always suspicious at places which didn't advertise their prices. Jenny giggled quietly and Purdy felt a little embarrassed that she'd said anything.

"No need to worry about prices here, it's all provided by The Facility, you just order whatever you like, you'll see there are no prices on anything here, it's all free."

"All free?" Purdy asked. She'd always lived by the ideal that nothing in life was free, you paid for it one way or another.

"Yes, it's great here, everything is provided, we want for nothing." Purdy considered this prospect. She wondered who exactly ran The Facility, she'd presumed that it was the government as she was being held in quarantine away from the general population but it seemed unprecedented that the government would provide this level of comfort and amenity for free. This was more like something the high tech companies like Google or Facebook provided to their staff to encourage them to stay longer hours at the office.

"Wow, it all looks pretty nice considering it's provided for free"

"Mmm hmm", Jenny was choosing her breakfast from the menu on the tablet, then she handed it to Purdy. Purdy looked down the extensive list, just like the options in the yellow room this menu was endless. She settled on an egg white omelette with vegetables, all the pancakes and take-out style food she'd been eating for the last few days had left her craving something light but filling. She pressed order and put the tablet back on the edge of the table.

"So, Purdy, right?" Purdy nodded, she knew it was an unusual name and she was impressed that Jenny had remembered it, often people would call her Patti or Penny and she was usually too polite to correct them. "So how long were you in isolation before they let you come over here?"

"Five days. It wasn't bad being in there for five days but I did miss the fresh air."

"Yeh it gets like that, huh? You're lucky, though, five days is a really good. Some have to stay for much longer than that."

"Oh they do?" Purdy thought about it, it made sense that different diseases would require different isolation periods to her she guessed "So how long did you have to stay in there?"

"Oh I was in there a little longer, no big deal. Listen, there are some things you should know so as not to get in trouble" She used air quotes as she said 'get in trouble'. "The Facility has a rule, you don't talk about why you are in here, it's a respect of privacy thing."

"Get in trouble?" Purdy echoed, what trouble could she get in and with whom?

"Yeh there's just a few rules, you know, to keep this a great place to be. You're expected to respect everybody else and not pry into their lives. You're not to burden others with information about your life."

"Look I don't expect to be here..." Jenny interrupted Purdy before she could get her sentence out by holding her hand up.

"Shh!" she spat at Purdy "I told you, you're not to share these things with anyone. I don't need to know your plans, where you've been or where you are going and you don't need to know that information about anyone else here, understand? It's just not worth the consequences."

"Consequences? What consequences? Look this all sounds a little bit too strange to me. I'm only here.." Purdy was starting to think that she may have misjudged Jenny and she was actually a bit of a nut job after all.

"Strange it may be but I'm telling you, keep yourself to yourself and things will be better for everyone."

Jenny interrupted her again and Purdy was now convinced that this Jenny was a bit of a crazy, and she wasn't sure what else she could talk about.

"Erm, ok. Am I allowed to ask if you know where we are? All I see is hills and green fields for miles around, I'm not used to this scenery and I'm just wondering where geographically we are." Purdy stopped short of saying she was in San Francisco before she came here as that might be breaking the new rule she'd just been told. Even if the rule was odd, it was not in Purdy's nature to break rules she'd been told, if nothing else Purdy was a rule follower and until she found out what these 'consequences' were she wasn't about to risk it.

"Of course! We're in The Facility" god, it was like pulling teeth with this woman.

"Riiight, and The Facility is in which city?" Purdy thought she'd try a different line of questioning, after all she was a lawyer, witness questioning was something she'd been trained to do.

"Well it's not in a city, it's like a city in itself." curiouser and curiouser thought Purdy, she did feel a little like Alice when she fell down the rabbit hole after all.

"Presumably we are still in California though, right?" Leading the witness? Jenny nodded in agreement and a robo-waiter appeared with their food. Just the same as the yellow room everything looked and smelt delicious. They retrieved their meals from the robo-waiter and began to tuck in. Again, the food tasted delicious, everything Purdy had eaten since she'd been here had tasted like the best version of that dish she had ever tasted, maybe it was all the fresh air out here.

They ate in silence for a while, Purdy wasn't really sure what they could talk about so she was waiting for Jenny's cue and considering different ways to tackle the questions around "where are we" and "what consequences for breaking the rules". And on that note, were these rules written down somewhere so she could make sure not to break them or would she just have to hope she didn't break a rule inadvertently? She felt she should be more concerned about these things but this food was just so delicious it was distracting her from thinking too deeply about it.

"So what do you like to do for fun? There are all sorts of ways to entertain yourself here from amateur dramatics to the gym, we have everything!" Jenny's enthusiastic question broke the silence.

"I like VRing, reading, I like to go to the gym…"

"We have all those things here for you to enjoy! I can't wait to show you. The gym is next door, you probably noticed it? It has everything, it even has a pool out back, do you like to swim?" Purdy nodded slowly, she liked to but if there were a load of other quarantined people in here who she wasn't allowed to ask what they were here for she wasn't sure she wanted to take a chance swimming with them, they thought she had TB after all, what if someone else showed signs of polio, she was pretty sure she'd heard that was spread by water, she might end up getting sick here when she came in with no illness; maybe she was just being paranoid though. "Oh good, the pool is lovely, it's as big as an olympic pool and the water is perfect. In the upstairs rooms of the gym are the VRing studios, they're pretty popular but if you enjoy that you should sign up for some sessions."

Some sessions, the words echoed in her head. It was sounding more and more to Purdy like Jenny assumed she was going to be here for a while, she looked around and wondered how long other people had been here, but she daren't ask. She hoped to meet someone other than Jenny soon, maybe they would be more willing to let her in on this secretive place. Then the thought was gone, shrugged off with another mouthful of her mouthwatering omelette.

After breakfast Jenny offered to take Purdy for a tour of the gym next door. In the absence of any other pressing engagements Purdy took her up on the offer, she was intrigued to see more of this place.

Jenny wasn't wrong when she'd said that the gym had everything. Purdy looked around at the vast room of machines stretching out in front of her. As far as the eye could see were ellipticals, steppers, rowing machines and treadmills. In the distance she could make out weight machines as well as free standing dumbbells. She was impressed by how well equipped the place was, she'd genuinely never seen anything like it.

All around her were people working out, some of them had projected monitors in front of their machines, wearing ear buds and watching shows or listening to music. Most were engrossed in what they were doing, solitary pursuits, lost in their own thoughts or the videos they were watching. As they walked towards the weights area she noticed that there were pairs of people helping each other out, spotting each other while they used the heavy weights.

Just as they were outside, the people in here were dressed identically only the uniform in here came in various guises. Again it was either all black or all blue and the occasional person who was part of a pair was dressed all in red but there were various items of clothing. Some wore yoga pants, some sweat pants and others wore shorts. Tops ranged from sweaters to t shirts to tank tops but all in identical hues. She wondered if the people in red could be trainers, that would maybe explain why they were always part of a pair and none were alone.

They walked all the way through the gym and got to a large door which opened as they approached. Behind it was an enormous aqua marine pool. The water was crystal clear and sparkled from sunlight which came through windows high on the wall beyond. It was mesmerizing, quite stunning, one of the most inviting looking pools Purdy had ever set eyes on. Right there and then she felt almost compelled to run over and dive into it. Her concerns over what disease her fellow inhabitants may be harboring quickly dissolved, here was a place she could come and get lost in her own thoughts, swim and swim for as long as she desired or had the energy to, with not a care in the world.

She would have just stayed staring had Jenny not pulled her away in an excited hurry to show her the VRing studios upstairs. She made a promise to herself to come back here later, on her own. They went up a wide staircase at the side of the room. At the top was a touch screen, similar to the ticket machine at the Augmented Reality Studios in San Francisco, only with no requirement to make payment. It seemed you just picked your experience and then you go into one of the studios as long as they were free. Purdy counted 10 individual doors from where she was standing, she presumed there was one studio behind each door but she was sure she heard Jenny say there were 40 studios in total so maybe she was only seeing a small section of them. All the studios were being used according to the touch screen but there was a place to sign up, as Jenny had suggested earlier so Purdy considered putting her name down. She stopped herself, after all she wouldn't be here for long and it seemed wrong to take up a space someone else might be able to use.

When the tour of the gym was over they stepped outside into the sunshine again. Purdy looked across the square and took in the huge blue building which housed her room, the "Blue Mansion" as Jenny had called it. It was quite magnificent, she kind of understood the mansion moniker, it looked quite grand and of course it was blue. It was well looked after with what looked like a new paint job and had very clean windows. She wondered who did all the cleaning around here, they did a great job. She looked at the white and the red buildings, identical in every way but color. The White Mansion and the Red Mansion? She mused quietly to herself. She thought about asking Jenny but she was a bit fed up with her now, all she did was talk and talk and talk and really say nothing at all of interest so she decided against it, she didn't care enough to know the answer right now.

"Well! That's the grand tour done! What did you think? Isn't it all just amazing?!" Jenny was excitedly looking at Purdy, waiting for her response. Once again, her enthusiasm just was a little too much for Purdy who struggled to find the words to answer.

"Erm... well yes... it's all quite good, isn't it? You know, for a Facility..."

"It's the best place ever! I just love it here!" Jenny beamed. "I'm going to have to leave you for now, I have things to do but if you like we can meet for lunch?"

Lunch? They'd only just finished breakfast, she couldn't think about lunch just yet, but then again she felt she couldn't turn this woman down, she was, after all, the only contact she had made so far, best to put up with her for now until she got the lay of the land.

"Uh, sure. Shall I meet you in the Cafe? What time?"

"How about noon?"

"Sounds good, see you then"

"Cool, see you there, enjoy your morning!" Jenny was already walking away from Purdy and Purdy felt a great sense of relief. Finally some peace and quiet to take in the newness of it all.

What to do

Purdy had made her way back to the middle of the square, she sat on one of the few benches left that did not already have people sat on it, opposite the colossal fountain. She stared at the falling water, gushing and hitting the pool below loudly and pondered her situation. Six days ago she had just been going about her normal business, working, VRing and chatting with friends. Friends! Of course! She pulled her phone out of her pocket to see if she had much of a signal out here. She found it a little odd that it had taken her so long to think of her friends and her real life but now that she had she couldn't wait to talk to them. She dialed Fred... waited... number not available. Aargh! So annoying! She sent Fred a message: MESSAGE FRED: OK, SO BAD NEWS. I'M GOING TO BE STUCK HERE FOR A LITTLE LONGER. I'M NOT SURE HOW LONG BUT AT LEAST I'VE BEEN MOVED OUT OF ISOLATION AND AM NOW IN THIS WEIRD BUT PRETTY PLACE WITH A BIG FOUNTAIN AND AN EPIC GYM. WILL KEEP YOU UPDATED. MAYBE I'LL USE THIS TIME TO WORK ON MY FITNESS! HOPE ALL GOOD WITH YOU.

She watched the message fly off on her screen and noted it was delivered. She watched to see if there would be a response soon, no reply. It was unlike Fred, he usually answered in a flash but since she'd been here, at The Facility, he'd taken his time in answering all of her messages. Maybe he was busy she shrugged to herself and put her phone back in her pocket. Her attention once again taken by the gushing water, she stared as it streamed down.

After some time she looked around her. There seemed to be more people now but this was such a huge place it didn't seem at all crowded, no one was really paying any attention to her, which she was quite comfortable to see. They were all either staring at the fountain themselves or were deep in conversation with each other. She took in the array of people who were here with her. People of all colors, all dressed in blue or black, nothing to distinguish between them. No, wait, that was wrong, actually she noticed all the people dressed in black were women. She looked around to see if she could find any men dressed in black but no, all women. And not only that, but a lot of those women appeared to be in various stages of pregnancy. How odd, why would you put pregnant women in here with people who were quarantined?

Purdy was puzzled. She took a closer look at all of the people, not just the women in black but those wearing blue too to see if she was going mad or this was indeed the case. The people in blue were both men and women. There didn't appear to be any pregnant women in blue, but then again that's not surprising, it's not like great proportions of the general population were pregnant at the same time, why expect to see pregnant women in here? It was only the women in black who had made her wonder this. Maybe they were from a special quarantine group, maybe they were quarantined for the safety of their babies, although Purdy wasn't sure that that made sense but she was feeling confused over the whole situation, her eyes were drawn back towards the fountain again.

Suddenly she was aware that someone was sat on the bench next to her. She wasn't sure how long they had been sat there as they just seemed to appear, she slowly turned to look at them. It was man, a young man, maybe in his late twenties, wearing the same blue outfit that she had on. He looked back at her, a pleasant expression on his face.

"Hello!" he said cheerily.

"Uh hi..." Purdy replied, annoyed by his presence and not wishing to encourage him to stay around, she looked back towards the fountain.

"I'm Chuck" he persevered.

"Purdy"

"That's unusual!" he said, she didn't reply. "Haven't seen you before, are you new here?"

Purdy contemplated his question, was this breaking the "rules" she wondered, she answered shortly "Kind of, I suppose".

"Kind of, you suppose... ok. Did you have any questions you needed help with? I saw you in the gym earlier, are you planning a workout?" wow this guy was nosy.

"Maybe, I haven't really thought about it much."

"Well if you needed help with anything in there you just let me know, I know how all the machines work." This guy was weirdly helpful and dull all at the same time.

"Great, thanks, I'll bear that in mind." then it occurred to her he might be able to help with a pressing concern "Actually, I *was* wondering something; if I wanted to use the pool where could I get a swim suit from?" Chuck's face brightened, finally something he could be helpful with.

"Oh that's easy, just press your green button and ask. Same if you need any workout clothes, just press and ask, it's easy to get anything you need in here." Anything but internet connection she thought to herself.

"Oh ok, thanks." it seemed Chuck wasn't going to leave anytime soon and she was done with small talk for the day, Jenny had worn her out. "well, you know what then, I think I'm going to go back to my room and ask for a swimsuit then, thanks again for your help."

Purdy stood up and made towards the Blue Mansion.

"See you later!" Chuck called after her, shouting to be heard above the fountain. She turned and nodded at him, hoping that her face didn't betray her real desire which was not to bump into him again anytime soon.

When she got back to her room she was surprised to see a swim suit folded up and left on the desk for her. It was, unsurprisingly, a blue one piece suit, it wouldn't have been her first choice had she had a choice but it would do. The suit was accompanied by a large blue swim towel with instructions that this was to be left in the changing rooms at the pool after use and a clean one would be supplied to her room afterwards. It was always good not to worry about your own laundry so she appreciated this.

She slipped the swim suit on, and it fit perfectly. She considered why it had just appeared in her room with the towel, how did The Facility know that she was going to ask for a swim suit? She quickly dismissed the thought and presumed they probably left these items for everyone just in case, the same as the clothes were all left in the closet ready for her use. She pressed the green button to ask for some workout clothes, stating her preference for yoga pants and a t-shirt, and was assured they would be delivered momentarily. Within 15 minutes a drone appeared at the door with the delivery, she certainly appreciated the efficient and helpful service in this place.

She made her way back over to the gym. There were still a lot of people milling around. So this is what its like when no one has a job she mused to herself, go anywhere you like and do anything you want no matter what time of the day it is, maybe staying here really wasn't so bad, especially as it was all free. She found the changing rooms and came out poolside, again captivated by the aquamarine water she was thrilled to see that there were only 3 other people taking advantage of this wonderful, enormous pool and she had an entire olympic sized lane all to herself. She couldn't remember the last time she had been to the gym to use the pool and not had to worry about sharing a lane with someone else, trying to pace them, whether they be too slow and hindering her workout or too fast and wearing her out to the point of slow down and leaving her in their angry wake as they lapped her. There never seemed to be the right paced swimmer to share a lane with in her experience. She dived into the water in one of the clear lanes, the temperature was perfect and it felt good to be active.

One of the best things about swimming, apart from the weightlessness and the ease through which she could glide through the water was it was a solitary activity. She found she could swim for lengths and lengths and no one even attempted to interact with her, she thought she'd finally found her bliss. Alone and lost in her own thoughts. Not that she had that many thoughts to ponder. She found herself in this strange place but she felt she had nothing to complain about, so far she was being treated well and she felt a lot happier than she had done in who knows how long. Maybe it was the novelty of the place, it would likely wear off soon enough. Her thoughts turned to her friends, she wondered what they were doing, working probably. Work, yes she found she didn't miss work at all in reality, struggling to recall what it was that she did really. Sat at a desk, staring at a screen and handing out common sense advice to others, she doubted anyone even missed her presence, it wasn't like they couldn't get the information from anyone else, no she did not miss work. It was odd, though, not having had a conversation with her boss about not being around and who would cover, she just couldn't find the energy to care about it, she put it to the back of her mind to worry about another time.

She lost track of time in the pool and soon noticed it was almost noon, time to meet Jenny again. Although the prospect of more small talk with Jenny didn't thrill her she still thought it was best not to isolate herself completely from other people whilst she was here. She left the pool and went to meet her lunch companion at the cafe. She was anxious but somewhat curious when she realized Jenny was standing outside with two other people waiting for her. Another woman and a man, they both looked a similar age to Purdy. Who knows one or both of them might be interesting to talk to, she had nothing to lose by finding out after all.

Georgia and Derek were their names. Both of them were pleasant enough but confirmed Jenny's warning from breakfast was true, she really knew very little about either of them even after sharing a table with them for an hour in the cafe because they weren't "allowed" to share information about why they were here or where they were from, or what their future plans were for that matter. So all she had learnt about them was that Derek loved spending his days in the theater with the others who fancied themselves as thespians, rehearsing and performing plays and Georgia was a fitness fanatic.

Apparently there was a group who did rehearsed plays daily called the "Company" and every so often they performed the plays publicly in the theater. She had not been shown the theater yet but it turned out that it was on the ground floor of the building marked Art, which she'd not paid much attention to before hearing about the plays. It briefly crossed her mind that surely people weren't in here long enough to get involved in such activities, rehearsing must take weeks but again she was discouraged from asking the question and it felt unnecessary anyway once Derek started talking so passionately about the play he was currently working on, which she promised she would come to watch when they performed it, whether or not she would be still here by then was another matter which seemed unimportant.

Georgia was a gym bunny, spending her days running endlessly on the treadmill and taking yoga classes (yoga, pilates and zumba classes were led by instructors on projected screens in the gym, who knows where the instructors actually were but Purdy suspected they refused to actually come into the room where the quarantined folks were, she didn't blame them). Georgia was super fit and ate like a horse, Purdy admired her somewhat but wondered what the heck she did outside of here that afforded her the time to keep up with that amount of exercise, of course maybe Georgia was a trainer or something physical, fire fighter maybe? It was kind of fun not knowing people's real backgrounds, it was more interesting to just make it up.

After lunch (once again, delicious, who *were* the chefs here? She wondered. This was some of the best food she'd ever had in her life) she went back to her room to watch a movie on her own and took a nap. She'd agreed to meet the others for dinner (life in here was very food driven, she was going to have to spend more time in that gym and pool just to keep healthy) and after her nap she took a walk around the square just to get her bearings.

The square was in fact huge and it took at least 30 minutes to walk the entire way around it. She passed people, some smiled, some said hello, she'd started to relax a little and returned smiles and nodded at people. She took note again that it was only ladies wearing black and they seemed to stick with each other. The people in blue mingled with each other too and no one wearing red seemed to make it out here to the square, maybe red was only to be worn in the gym if you were working out with someone else? The red clothes were quite nice, she wondered to herself how she might get hold of some of them.

Her walk took her to the door of the Art building, the door opened as she approached it and she stepped inside. There was a screen on the wall which pointed her in the direction of the theater. She noted the other rooms in the building; Painting, Drawing, Ceramics, Sewing, Knitting, so many rooms filled with people creating art. It was funny, she thought to herself, that she never saw the fruits of those labors, this place was kept neat and tidy and it looked spic and span but there was no art to be seen (other than the ornate fountain) and no variety in clothing with everyone wearing the same uniforms in the three distinct colors.

Once again there were robo-waiter style robots in there either cleaning or docked by the walls. No drones but she wondered if this was maybe where the drones were kept when they weren't flying around delivering things. She'd got used to the sound of them now as they were constantly flying around. When drones first became mainstream she remembered her first experience of one coming over her backyard. She had been stood in the doorway drinking a cup of tea and breathing in the fresh morning air when she'd heard what sounded like a swarm of bees coming towards her. She couldn't see anything but she ducked inside the door as they sounded aggressive, the next thing she knew a drone had appeared over the fence and was flying across her yard. She almost spilt her tea when she jumped in fright at the idea she was about to be attacked by the swarm and then giggled to herself whilst she hid inside from the drone. She had no idea who it had belonged to but suspected it had a camera and felt a little violated it had appeared in her yard when she was stood there in her pyjamas. Times had moved on since then and drones were completely the norm now, they also had worked on making them quieter, they weren't as loud as they had been back then but you could still for the most part hear them coming.

With nothing else keeping her interest in the Art building and with the knowledge that it was almost dinner time she stepped out of the door and made her way to the cafe. Walking towards her was Chuck, the guy from the fountain this morning. He smiled as he approached her.

"Hello again!" he said cheerily "Did you get your swim suit?"

Feeling less annoyed by him this time Purdy returned his smile "yes, thanks, and thanks for the information earlier, I did appreciate it."

"Of course, anytime. Got to dash, you have a fun evening!" and with that he scuttled off and into the Art building.

Maybe he wasn't that bad really, at least he just seemed helpful and pleasant. Everyone she had come across in here was. They were all in the same boat, she supposed, so what was the point in not being friendly to each other, this wasn't their lives after all, just a brief encounter before they rejoined the real world.

The others were already at the Cafe and she joined them at the table. Another sumptuous meal and then Purdy was ready for some alone time. They parted ways and she walked slowly back to her room, past the fountain, in the early evening dusk it was lit by blue light from below and looked quite marvelous. She passed it slowly taking it all in, whoever pays for this place doesn't skimp, she thought, it's really like a nice resort, when she got back to her room she planned to press the green button and ask how much longer she would be here. By the time she got there she'd forgotten all about this and just settled down in bed with a book she had requested earlier before falling into a deep and restful slumber.

A break from the routine

Each day passed in much the same way; three meals a day with the same three people, swimming, walking the grounds and spending time alone in her room reading or watching movies and shows. Each day it ran through her head to ask about when she would get to leave and each day the desire to leave left her a little more, and it got to the point where the days had all melded into each other she couldn't even recall how long she had been there. In actual fact twelve weeks had passed but to the contented Purdy it seemed only a couple of weeks.

This was her life. She'd long forgotten her job, her friends and her cute San Francisco house. After the first couple of days while she was getting used to her new surroundings she'd sent a couple of messages to Fred and received one in reply, since then she'd felt no desire to reach out to him and it seemed he had no desire to contact her either. She'd had no communication at all with Flo since moving into the Blue Mansion. Her phone had been left on her desk charging but she only ever picked it up when she wanted to read one of the books she borrowed, it no longer occurred to her to use it as an actual phone anymore. But she was very content.

Happy with her lot. Secure in her routine, and the freedom she felt she had to go anywhere at anytime within The Facility as she pleased, never even considering if she could leave and if not, why not, it was as though she suppressed the idea because she was so comfortable now that it filled her with fear to not be inside her new, safe home.

Today was the first time she was going to do something out of that ordinary routine, today was the opening night of Derek's play. The Company had been rehearsing three one act plays and tonight they were showcasing all three of them for the inhabitants of The Facility - Derek had got tickets for Purdy, Jenny and Georgia to come and watch him, he was the lead in one of the plays and was super excited with his chest all puffed out in pride, this was Derek in his element it seemed.

Derek didn't join them for dinner as he usually did because he was off at a last minute technical rehearsal where, as he had knowingly informed the others, the technical crew of The Company checked that the light and sound was all working correctly before the big opening night. It all sounded like such a professional operation that Purdy was thrilled to see what the theater was like as she hadn't had the chance to see inside it yet; of course presuming it was like the rest of The Facility it would be pretty amazing, as good as any Broadway or West End theater, no doubt.

The ladies excitedly discussed the evening ahead over dinner without him. They were looking forward to seeing their friend up on stage strutting his stuff, although Purdy shared her concern about how they would react if he turned out to be terrible. They all agreed, even though it seemed unlikely, if it turned out that Derek was not actually very good they would all just smile and tell him they really enjoyed it. Purdy felt lucky to have met such a nice bunch of people, she had long forgotten how irritating she'd found Jenny when they first met, now she just seemed so lovely and enthusiastic about everything, Purdy found it too hard not to like her.

After dinner they headed over the Art building. A big crowd of people were filing in the same direction, it seemed these one act play nights were popular. They moved along inside with the crowd and just outside the theater door was a group of ladies in black outfits taking tickets and showing people where they were to sit inside. The lady who took Purdy's ticket was quite heavily pregnant, she looked ready to pop, but she smiled kindly at Purdy and told her she hoped she enjoyed the show, even though she looked like standing here dealing with all these people was probably quite a chore at this stage. Purdy thanked her and walked into the theater.

The auditorium was quite breathtaking. It looked exactly like a theater in London which Purdy had once attended to watch Sheridan's The Rivals many, many years ago. She was surprised at the clarity of the memory she had about that play and the smells and sounds that came flooding back to her. In that briefest of brief moments she was suddenly mournful for the life she once had, before The Facility, before she even moved to the US and then as quickly as it arrived the memory left her and she was just left to gaze around in awe at this amazingly decorated theater with no recollection of that earlier time. Dramatic tapestries hung from the high ceiling which was covered in a large mural, spectacular vistas were painted on the walls and statues sat in elevated places throughout. The stage was large and heavy red velvet curtains hung there, hiding the platform behind where the actors would perform. It looked old with an antique feel to it but at the same time it seemed brand new.

They took their seats, they were the red velvet covered flip kind that were found in most theaters. Georgia knew from visiting the theater before that there was a refreshment stand at the back of the auditorium, so she'd offered to go and bring back snacks and drinks for all of them. It felt like such an adventure. Jenny and Purdy sat in their seats and looked through the playbill they had been handed when they walked in. Derek was listed as the lead in the last of the three plays they were to see, if the other two were bad, sadly they had to sit through them for Derek's sake, they both hoped for at least watchable if good wasn't an option.

Georgia returned from the refreshment stand with a tray of drinks and her pockets stuffed with snacks.

"Just as I thought!" she beamed at the others "Red wine! I got us a glass each, hope that works for everyone!"

Purdy gladly took the red wine from her friend, she wasn't a wine connoisseur by any stretch of the imagination and genuinely couldn't recall the last time she had indulged in red wine but she presumed it would have to be good stuff, everything was at The Facility after all, and it seemed rude not to join in with the festivities! Jenny declined saying it gave her a headache but urged the other two to share her glass between them. Jenny gladly took a bottle of water that Georgia pulled out of her pocket instead, along with the candy that was proffered. Happily they all settled down with their snacks and drinks and awaited the curtain up.

The first play was a comedy and was delivered quite well, it caused a few laughs and they enjoyed it well enough, all that might have been down to the initial glow from the glass and a half of wine that Purdy had been drinking though. She was having a wonderful old time and it was fun to see people wearing the costumes, clothes other than the blue, black and red uniforms that she was used to seeing for once was quite a welcome change. One of the characters was wearing a little black dress and again Purdy's memory threw her a brief recollection of a dress she had worn years ago on a blind date she'd once been encouraged to go on by Fred... Fred! And as quickly as that the memory appeared it was gone again, Fred was forgotten, pushed back to the recesses of her mind.

The lights came up in the interval between the first and second plays. A lot of the people around them were getting up and moving around, likely taking bathroom trips and replenishing their refreshments. The three friends stayed in their seats, chatting animatedly about the play and how they enjoyed it, what they would have liked to have seen that would have made it better and so on. Purdy was laughing at something Georgia had said, feeling a little giddy from the wine. She turned away to grab half a bag of M&Ms that was slipping from her lap as she giggled uncontrollably, her gaze suddenly fell on a familiar face across the aisle and she took a sharp intake of breath, almost immediately stopping her giggles. The face was familiar but Purdy couldn't place where she had seen it before. The owner of the face smiled at her and made an attempt at a wave, Purdy felt embarrassed and looked away, who was that man and where did she recognize him from? She looked back and he was still looking, still with a slight smile and what seemed to be a look of hope on his face, she raised the briefest of smiles at him and looked away again, still unsure of who he was or how she might know him.

Her friends were still chatting away but Purdy was now lost in her own thoughts, desperately searching her memory banks for any signs of who he might be but to no avail, nothing was coming to her.

"Hey! You OK?" Georgia was nudging her.

"Yeh, fine thanks..." she murmured. Georgia gave her a weird look as if she didn't believe her but she wasn't going to press her on the subject and she went back to her discussion with Jenny.

Purdy looked back over the aisle again but the man has disappeared. She sat back in her chair and contemplated where she knew him from. It occurred to her that she might have seen him in the pool and maybe he just looked different dried out and fully dressed which would explain why she was finding it hard to place him. He was a handsome looking man, maybe she had just noticed him around and she'd thought him somehow appealing so now he was stuck somewhere in her brain. The lights went down for the second play to begin and Purdy was soon engrossed in the drama that unfolded on the stage; the man drifted out of her immediate thoughts and back into the fog of her memories.

The second play wasn't as good as the first but they had high hopes for the final play with Derek in the lead role. Georgia dashed off just before the second play ended to get them some more drinks and snacks, she came back with two more glasses of red. Purdy tried to protest that she'd really had enough but Georgia had become quite insistent that it would be rude to leave her to drink alone so Purdy had relented and accepted she could drink another glass after all. Georgia had more snacks in her pockets and Jenny was delighted she'd brought back some popcorn too.

The wine was taking effect and Purdy's head was a swimming a little, she thought it best if she just re-mained seated and started sipping on the water that Georgia had also brought back with her. She was staring at the stage but felt like her right eye was going a little cross-eyed at odds with her left eye so nothing looked normal, she closed them both and hoped when she reopened them things would seem a little better. The lights went down again and Derek's play began, he walked out onto the stage dressed in a tuxedo, Purdy was intrigued and squinted at the stage through one eye, it would be a shame to miss Derek's play now after they'd sat through the other two. She took some slow deep breaths and sipped on the water, she could do this, she was sure.

The play was over in forty-five minutes, luckily it was funny and entertaining so Purdy managed to ignore that she felt unwell as it was a good distraction. When the show finished they stood up and clapped loudly, cheering for Derek to come out and take a bow which he of course did with a theatrical flourish, he was lapping up the attention of his adoring crowd. Georgia and Jenny were going to wait for Derek to get changed and walk back to the Blue Mansion with him. Purdy, still feeling a little worse for wear, decided she wanted to go and lie down so she bid them farewell and asked them to congratulate Derek on a job well done from her. Jenny offered to walk back with her but Purdy declined the kind offer, she was concerned she might actually throw up and couldn't stand the humiliating thought that someone might see her, or even offer to hold her hair like she was some naive teen having her first taste of hard liquor and not knowing her limits.

As she walked out of the door to the Art building the air hit her like a new wave of alcohol had hit her blood stream. Immediately she was dizzy again and having difficulty focusing her eyes. She could see the Blue Mansion across the square and decided to take the most direct route she could in a straight line past the fountain. It was already dark outside and the fountain was lit up from below, letting off a blue haze around it. There were people sat on benches watching the water and a couple of them said hi as she walked past. She managed a smile at each of them, at least she hoped her mouth was making a smile, in honesty she'd lost all feeling in her face at this point and she could just be staring at them like a deranged person. Just as she got to the loudest part of the fountain there he was again, the man from the theater. He smiled at her and opened his mouth to speak. The water was so loud she couldn't hear what he was trying to say and she was just trying to get back to her room quickly before she embarrassed herself so she quickened her pace and moved away from him.

She reached the door and glanced over her shoulder to see if he was behind her. It seems he hadn't tried to follow her and she felt a mix of relief and disappointment at this. She shook her head, she was sure she would see him again and once she was sober she might even be able to remember him. She got to her room just in time, flying through the bathroom door and lifting the lid of the toilet seat in time to wretch into the bowl. Three more times and she was completely empty, all the snacks, wine and dinner removed from her stomach. She laid down on the floor with the cool tile on her cheek. Lucky those drones come in and clean daily, she thought to herself, her bathroom at home had never been this clean. That thought of home left pangs of emptiness in her heart but once again the thought was fleeting and soon she was asleep on the floor of the bathroom, dreading how she might feel when she eventually woke up.

Who is he?

Purdy stirred from her sleep. During the night she'd stumbled her way from the bathroom floor and crawled into her bed and she was grateful to wake up surrounded by a comforting duvet. Her head had a mild throb to it and her tummy gurgled its disapproval at the previous night's wine consumption. Purdy leant over and pressed her green button, requesting a couple of bottles of water, water being all she could face right now. Within minutes a drone appeared with two ice cold bottles of Smart water and she took them with great appreciation.

She laid in her bed, cracked the seal from one of the bottles and delicately took a few sips of the icy cold liquid whilst sifting through her hazy memories. She recalled the red wine that Georgia had brought to her and then wondered why she had accepted it so readily, red wine had always had this effect on her and she never drank it usually. Usually. Again her thoughts skipped to her life in the outside world, outside of The Facility, this time the thought was clearer and lasted a little longer. What was she doing here? How long had it been and when would she be getting out? The questions would remain unanswered as the thoughts flittered away again like butterflies on a sunny day.

She had slept for a long time, breakfast time had come and gone and she didn't feel well enough to attempt to eat anyway. She considered going for a swim but dismissed the idea as foolhardy, swimming would not help with the way she was struggling to control her inner temperature and her unsettled stomach. It seemed quite ambitious to even try and jump in the shower but she struggled with all her might because she was sure it would help her to feel a little better.

She stood for about 20 minutes in the shower, it reminded her of the very first day she was here, when she was in the yellow hell, funny she'd not thought about that place much at all since moving into the Blue Mansion. She recalled that shower, with her sore arms and aching body, she rubbed her upper arms with her hands and noticed that the lump was still there in her left arm from the tetanus shot. Not a big lump but certainly a noticeable bump under the skin. It was the first time she'd paid attention to it since that first day. Her head was still pounding slightly and it made her thoughts scramble a little but she desperately tried to hang on to the curiosity over why she hadn't been paying attention to these things but again the thoughts quickly disappeared and she went back to just enjoying the warm, steady stream of water cascading over her body.

She took her time getting dressed after her shower while contemplating what she should do to help clear her head. Swimming still was out of the question so she settled on a walk in the fresh air. Her mum had always been a huge proponent of taking a walk in the fresh air to blow away the cobwebs, she stopped and realized she'd not thought of her mum, or her dad for that matter, since being here. She was overwhelmed momentarily by a sense of grief which now felt alien to her, a grief she had felt since she lost them that infiltrated each and every defining moment she'd had in her life. The sadness that they weren't there to share in her success or support her in her failures, her eyes filled with tears and then once again the feeling and memory was lost.

It was a bright sunny day outside so she routed around in her handbag for a pair of sunglasses she was pretty sure she recalled carrying in there, she couldn't face bright sunshine without them. Bingo! She found them along with a number of other items she'd forgotten she had, a pack of gum, her passport (it had her visa in it and, ever the rule follower, she never went anywhere without it), and a small notepad with a pencil attached. Since everyone carried a phone or phablet with them these days it was rare anyone had a need for a pencil and paper but Purdy liked to doodle when she sat in on conference calls and always found it easier to do this with a pencil than using her finger or a stylus no matter how good they had become. She looked at the pad, the first couple of pages had her doodles on them. Then she turned to a page with a question mark on it. She looked at it, it seemed to be her writing but she didn't recall writing it, she briefly considered it then shrugged, closed the notepad and dropped it back in her bag.

She walked out into the square with her sunglasses shielding her from the bright day. As was usual, people were sitting around in the square chatting with each other and walking with purpose towards the Gym and the other buildings around the square. Purdy took it slowly, walking the perimeter of the square, smiling at people, not knowing who any of them were but she was now used to this, people here just acknowledged each other whenever they passed one another.

After a full circuit she felt a little better and walked to the middle of the square to take a seat opposite the fountain. As always she stared into the water, watching it gushing and swirling into the pool below. The view had a calming effect on her which made her relax helping her headache to drift away from her temples. She shut her eyes and the noise filled her ears calming her further still. She sat there steadily breathing in and out and enjoying the solitude.

Time passed and Purdy began to feel more human, the headache had lifted, the nausea was long gone and she was starting to feel peckish. She opened her eyes to check on the time. There, directly in front of her right by the fountain was the mysterious man from last night. She'd forgotten about him but there he was, the flashback from the night before of him smiling across the theater at her ran through her mind and her heart skipped a little. Who was this man she recognized but had no recollection of? He was sideways on, also looking at the fountain. She thought about calling out to him but wasn't sure how to address him, plus the fountain was so loud she wasn't sure he would hear. He didn't turn her direction, just continued looking at the water.

Purdy got to her feet, he still didn't turn so, feeling emboldened by his smile from the night before she approached him. As she got close to him, he still didn't move, maybe he was lost in his own thoughts. She hesitated but braveness took over.

"Hello?" she called out to him, she was close now, she needed to be in order to avoid having to shout over the noise of the fountain. He turned his head and smiled at her. He reached out and rested his hand on the top of her left arm. Usually she was someone very aware of her personal space but something about him made her feel safe, she didn't mind his touch and a shudder of pleasure ran through her body at the weight of his hand on her body.

"Hello" he said, moving close to her ear so as not to shout too loudly, "I was hoping you would remember me."

She studied his face and the sound of his voice, desperately searching the archives of her memory trying to recall where she knew him from. She felt disappointed at not being able to remember him and reluctant to admit it to him for fear he might remove his attention from her, which she was enjoying more than she would have expected. She had obviously been silent too long.

"You do remember me, don't you?" he asked looking a little crestfallen.

"I... I... I'm so sorry, I know I recognize you, I just can't put my finger on from where. But I'm having trouble with my memory at the moment so please don't take it personally, remind me of your name and I'm sure it will come back to me." she pleaded with him.

"Don't worry too much, we have only met once, its not surprising that you don't have as much recollection of me as I have of you, I've been looking for you."

He'd been looking for her? Looking for her where? Here? Had they met before in here? It was possible after all, maybe.

"My name is Ben." he offered. Ben, she thought to herself, Ben, she didn't know any Bens, did she? "Your car.." he started to say and a memory popped back into her mind. Of course! Ben, the mechanic. Ben the man who she accused of videoing her. Ben the man she humiliated herself in front of. The embarrassment of that moment flooded back to her at once and she wanted to run away. Her face flushed and his smile widened when he saw from her look that she was remembering him.

"You do remember!"

"I do, yes, vaguely" she managed. "Look, I'm really sorry…" she started to say.

"No, no. No need for apologies and no time for all that." No time? She thought, they were running out of time? She hadn't worried about time in so long.

"We can't talk for long. Just please, please try to remember me and keep me in your thoughts. We need to talk again."

Well this was all a bit cryptic, she thought, why couldn't they talk now?

"I need you to remember that I'm Ben. I need you to remember to meet me later. Please agree." he implored her.

"Ok, ok, you're Ben. When do you want to meet?" this was all very weird but frankly her entire life was weird right now so why should this be any different. Besides it was quite exciting, this attractive man wanting her to remember him stirred something inside her. She actually wanted to remember him, these were stronger feelings than she had had since arriving here and it was good to feel something again.

"I also need you to be careful about what you eat." What? This strange man who had just shown up in her life for the second time had some issue with what food she ate? How did he know? He was a mechanic, wasn't he? Was this some weird control thing? Some odd way of suggesting that she didn't care enough about what she put in her mouth, that she was in someway unhealthy? She started to protest but he cut her off "No, no it's very important." he said "Please, I'll explain later but for now, avoid protein as much as you can, stick to carbs and try to start your meals with a glass of milk."

Stick to carbs and drink milk? The opposite to what most diets in the early 21st century had encouraged everyone to do, but she could cope with that she supposed. Still she thought it was odd, why on earth would he be suggesting what she ate at all? On the other hand, any excuse to eat bread and french fries worked for her...

"Milk and no protein, ok got it - again, though, where and when shall we meet?"

"Right here, after dark, when the lights go blue, we can talk for longer then, ok?

"Ok" she nodded her agreement.

"I know I'm asking for a lot from you to just take me on trust, I understand if you're suspicious, especially after our last meeting but there will be time later for me to explain more, I promise" he looked at her hopefully and she nodded again, she was suspicious and confused but there was something about him, the memory of him, that put her at ease, she couldn't explain it but she felt a sense of tranquility in his company, and that was a rare thing in her experience. "And lastly, for your own sake, you can't tell anyone else you know me or are meeting me, do you understand?"

For my own sake? She thought to herself, more cryptic instructions! One the other hand, although she liked the people she'd made friends with on a superficial level in here, the inability to talk about their lives outside of The Facility had prohibited her from really, properly bonding with them, so she certainly didn't feel the need to immediately run and tell them about this Ben guy.

"OK, I understand, I won't say a word"

He beamed and let go of her arm, she felt slightly bereft at the loss of his touch. He began to walk away and she wanted any reason to make him stay. "Wait!" she called after him but he continued walking, maybe he hadn't heard her.

Trying to remember

Purdy went over to the Cafe to get some lunch. She saw her three friends all sat at a table and waved at them as she walked through the door. She had a certain frisson of excitement around her but she'd made up her mind to absolutely keep Ben to herself and not mention him to the others, not only because of his warning but because she didn't want to let anyone into her own little world, she wanted it to be just her thing, not for others to discuss and dissect with their opinions.

She was feeling so much better than this morning and was ready for a feast but Ben's food advice stuck in her head, start with milk and stick to carbs, hmm she wondered if they had French Toast on the menu today, she could polish that off quite easily.

"Morning Sleeping Beauty!" Georgia bellowed at her playfully, she had presumed Purdy must have a hangover and thought she'd have some fun with her.

"Yes, yes I know!" chuckled Purdy as she sat down, "Did I put on a shocking show last night? I'm sorry, I don't usually drink red wine as I can't handle it..."

"So we saw!" Jenny teased.

"I'm mortified, really I am!" Purdy blushed, "honestly, did I make a show of myself? All I recall is feeling woozy and having to get out of there. Derek! You were wonderful, by the way, I'm sorry I should have led with that! I loved your play."

"Oh sure, sure," Derek smirked "The way I heard it I doubt you even remember my play!"

Purdy smiled apologetically and picked up the tablet to order her lunch. That was weird, this menu was pretty renowned for having everything on it but she couldn't find a glass of milk anywhere. She opted for ordering a cup of tea and specifying she wanted milk to go in it and ordered the French toast.

"French toast?! You missed breakfast you know!" Jenny poked at her "And milk for your tea? Who drinks milky tea?"

"It's the only thing I can handle when I feel a little off color" Purdy thought quickly, she wasn't sharing the news of Ben and in turn there would be no talk of the new diet guidelines she was adhering to "well, you know I *am* British, its the *only* way one should drink tea, hot with milk!"

The others looked uncomfortable at her mention of being British, oh sure they could tell from her accent that she was but it went against The Facility rules to speak of such things. Purdy gulped at her faux pas and looked down at the table, in her excitement she was forgetting herself, she must calm down.

"So…" she began "Did you enjoy your opening night, Derek?" thankfully this drew the attention away from the awkwardness of her last comment and Derek happily told her the story of his evening and the ins and outs of the backstage politics of The Company. Apparently Derek had to share a dressing room with other actors from the other two plays and they were a messy lot, leaving their costumes strewn around the place with no care.

Purdy's tea arrived as a teabag in a cup, a jug of hot water and a jug of milk. She took it from the robo-waiter and tried to not let the others see she pretty much just filled her cup with the milk and drank it quickly so they didn't notice the lack of hot water in her cup. Milk with a dry tea bag in it was not the best but it was the only way she could manage this without arousing suspicion. At least that is what she hoped. When she'd finished the cup of milk she poured some of the hot water into the cup to make the tea bag looked used and put the last dribble of milk in the cup, that way she hoped it looked like she had drunk a full cup of tea and just left the dregs in the bottom.

Her French toast arrived and it was superb. She rarely ate so decadently and she savored every mouthful, it had just the right amount of cinnamon flavoring and butter accompanying it. Purdy barely said a word to the others as she munched away on it, she was liking Ben more and more with every mouthful, any man who insisted her diet consisted of this was a top bloke in her books, of course it helped that he was pleasing to the eye too.

As she was feeling so much better she decided to go over and take a swim in the pool. After lunch she parted ways with the others and walked across the square to get her swimsuit. She was thinking about the swim and then it occurred to her that she couldn't remember Ben's name, the memory was swirling in her head and was in danger of leaving her completely, she stared at the fountain searching her mind. Ben! His name came to her. She didn't want to forget it again but wasn't sure how she could hold onto the thought. She broke into a run to get back to her room. She ran past a woman who looked startled at her demeanor, people didn't run here outside of the gym, Purdy contemplated slowing down to avoid any suspicion but feared she would forget Ben again.

"Sudden urge to pee!" Purdy called loudly enough for more people to turn around. How humiliating she thought to herself but it was the best she could come up with in the moment.

She ran into her room and pulled her notebook and pencil out of her bag. It happened that claiming she had the urge to pee had had the psychological effect of actually making her need to go so she skipped into the bathroom still carrying the pad and pencil. After she had dealt with her pressing bladder issue she wrote Ben on the page with the question mark. In case she forgot to open the pad again, which she feared may be a real possibility, she left it wedged under her toothbrush. She stood in the bathroom, still slightly out of breath from her dash and considered everything. Why did she keep forgetting everything? What was wrong with her? She was determined to sort herself out.

She grabbed her swimsuit and towel and went on over to the pool, a swim always made her feel refreshed and with the knowledge that she had the reminder on her pad about Ben she felt confident that she could enjoy it without having to desperately hang on to her thoughts which were quickly scrambling away from her.

Walking through the gym to get to the pool she glanced sideways at the people using the free weights, as usual they were in pairs. Mostly people in blue but the odd individual in red. All the usual blur of faces she didn't really recognize as she realized she didn't pay attention to the details ordinarily.

All of a sudden she did a double take, one of the people in red half smiled at her and gave her a brief wave. This time it was a face she did recognize, it was Chuck! The man who had been so helpful on her first day, she hadn't seen him since that first day but she was pretty sure he'd not been dressed in red, he was in blue the same as her. No one had ever confirmed it to her but she still assumed that the people in red were trainers as she really only saw them in the gym as part of a pair so she assumed Chuck was a trainer. That made sense, he had been so helpful on her first day and had offered to show her the machines in the gym. She waved back at him and thought he didn't look as cheerful as he did before, he looked away and spoke to the person he was with. She considered going over and asking if he was ok but he looked busy and she didn't want to interrupt so she continued on her way.

As was normal she had the a lane in the pool to herself and she swam and swam until her muscles were exhausted and her face burned from exertion. Her red wine fueled illness was long forgotten, as, sadly, was her meeting with Ben. She got dressed after her swim and immediately went to meet the others for dinner.

She found herself ordering pasta with a creamy sauce for dinner. This was unusual, not a dish she would normally go for but Jenny had picked it for herself and Purdy thought it sounded good. Along with the memory of Ben, the memory of her diet restrictions had flittered away but the fact that she ordered a pasta dish was maybe a sign that in someway she subconsciously remembered to eat carbs over protein.

Jenny and Purdy's dishes arrived at the same time on the same robo-waiter. Purdy reached over to take the plate closest to her at the same time as Jenny also grabbed that plate. Purdy giggled, but Jenny's demeanor changed.

"I want this one, let go" Jenny stared at her stony faced. Purdy wasn't generally one for fights over nonsense things and usually would let it go but she was surprised by Jenny's aggression and change of tone. She kept a hold of the dish closest to her and looked at the other one, the food was identical as far as she could see.

"There's no difference in them, why would you want this one?" Purdy hadn't taken kindly to Jenny's 'I want', those were the words of spoilt brat in her mind and she wasn't about to give into childish demands.

"I just want it."

"Well, 'I want's' don't get so why don't you just take the one closer to you?" Purdy was surprised at how firm she was on this matter, not one for conflict it felt a little empowering to stand up to Jenny when she was acting the brat. It seemed to take Jenny by surprise a little too. She let go of the dish and scowled at Purdy.

Another robo-waiter came along with drinks and Georgia and Derek's food, Georgia, who wasn't making eye contact with anyone due to the embarrassment of the scuffle over the pasta dishes quickly started rambling about how much she was looking forward to her dinner and shot Derek a look across the table to encourage him to join in.

Purdy took a spoon and started on her pasta, quietly pleased she'd won the battle but also confused about why there was ever a battle in the first place. Not wanting there to be any bad feeling between them, Purdy forced herself to make small talk and asked Jenny how her VRing was going, she'd been revisiting the same experience for a while as she tried to complete the level she was on. Jenny was still mad but seemed prepared to answer her questions. Interestingly she barely ate a thing, just kept pushing her pasta around her plate. Purdy thought she was mad, it was delicious but she felt she couldn't say that or she'd look like she was being ungracious so she didn't say a word about it but finished her whole bowl with satisfaction.

Full of food she decided to go back to her room and lie down, maybe watch a movie. She walked through the square, past the fountain on her way back to the Blue Mansion. The fountain made a memory flicker in her head like a streaming error during a show. The face of a man flickered in her head, a familiar but unnamed man, she'd seen him recently. The fountain, yes the fountain was where she had seen him but who was he. She stood there momentarily trying to recall. She felt it was important but it was fuzzy, what was wrong with her brain these days, she was starting to feel uneasy.

She quickly walked back to her room and sat on her bed. She stared at the desk. Noticing her phone, she picked it up and scrolled through it. No new messages. She contemplated sending Fred a message, nothing was stopping her, she just didn't know what to say. She looked at the conversation history between the two of them, he really didn't seem to be at all interested in where or how she was, why was that, it wasn't like him at all. All the messages they'd had were dull and routine, he was usually funny. Telling her funny stories, about his escapades but there was nothing, no sign of Fred at all in these messages. She sighed.

She wandered into the bathroom and noticed her notepad under the toothbrush. That's weird, she thought, how did that get there? She picked it up and just the feel of it stirred the memory in her, she wrote in it earlier! She opened the book and flicked through the pages, there on the third page was a question mark and the word Ben! Ben, that was him... Ben, who she was supposed to meet after dark at the fountain, handsome Ben who had been looking for her. Thank goodness she had remembered in time!

A Mystery Meeting

Purdy tried to tidy herself up a bit, in a bid to look her best for her meeting with Ben. It wasn't easy when her wardrobe only contained the same pieces of blue clothing over and over but she could at least tidy her hair up and she found her emergency make up fix kit in the bottom of her hand bag so managed to put on a little mascara to look like she'd at least made an effort to look presentable. She looked at herself in the bathroom mirror, satisfied with her reflection she put her make up away again.

When the sun started to set Purdy decided she'd go out into the square, it wasn't dark enough for the blue lights to come on yet but she liked to sit and watch the fountain anyway so she would sit and wait for Ben there. Excited at the prospect of meeting him she left her room in a hurry, as she turned to close the door she noticed Jenny was already in the corridor, quite close to Purdy's door, she jumped a little.

"Hi Jenny!" she exclaimed "Coming to see me?" she was concerned Jenny wanted to discuss the dinner incident and not only did she not like confrontation, especially over something so silly, she also didn't want to be held up for fear of missing Ben if this went on too long.

"No, I was just going over to do some VRing, where are you off to?"

Purdy thought quickly, she certainly wasn't going to tell Jenny about Ben right now as there wasn't time and she wasn't feeling that comfortable with Jenny's friendship since the pasta tussle either so she considered where she might be going at dusk that would not raise more questions.

"Oh, I was just going to go for a walk, it's a nice evening after all, and that pasta is still sitting in my tummy, thought a walk would do me good" Shit! Why did I mention the pasta, she thought to herself.

"I see," said Jenny, Purdy could tell she flinched at the memory of the pasta argument too. "Why don't we walk together, you can walk me to the Gym."

"Oh...Ok" Purdy nodded, grateful that there was no further discussion about the pasta and kicking herself a little for being so anxious to meet Ben that she'd left her room early and bumped into Jenny. At least she had time to walk with her to the gym though.

They walked out of the Blue Mansion together in silence. Purdy wasn't sure what to talk about, things between them were obviously strained.

"So which VRing experience are you doing right now, is it the same one you've been working on recently?" the silence was awkward, this was Purdy's attempt to lighten the mood.

"No, I'm trying a new one tonight" Jenny responded "They have added some new options and I saw this one earlier, thought I would give it a go."

Purdy nodded, waiting for her to expand further on what the new option was. Jenny explained that it was an adventure game where you were immersed in a fantasy world and had to complete challenges like taking potions from witches and stealing gold from dragons. Jenny went on and on about it and Purdy tuned her out, searching the square for Ben's face. She'd never been into the fantasy VRing, preferring to try real world experiences, but she continued to nod along whilst Jenny chatted away in an effort to appear as if she was paying attention. No sign of Ben, she was both disappointed and relieved. They were getting close to the gym door and Purdy began paying attention again to Jenny's chatter.

"So yeh, I thought I'd give it a go, it's a multiplayer game if you want to join me? Did I sell it to you?" Jenny was looking friendlier now but Purdy was not about to let herself be pulled into a fantasy game right now, she had more important things on her mind.

"Oh, thanks for the invite but I'll pass for now. I've never got into fantasy games really and I'm starting to feel a little sleepy, think I'll just go for a lap around the square and then head off to bed."

"OK then" Jenny shrugged "well, I'll see you tomorrow then!" and she went inside the gym.

Purdy stood alone in the square, happy that Jenny had left her and that maybe the awkwardness over dinner had disappeared. She walked back towards the fountain, it was almost dark now with no moonlight that she could see, the blue lights were yet to come on.

There were a few people milling around out here but it was generally quite quiet. There was more than one bench to pick from and Purdy went for the same one she had been sat on when she saw Ben by the fountain earlier that day. With the low level of light she couldn't really see the water very well, but she could hear it flowing and crashing loudly, she found the sound soothing and briefly closed her eyes. The blue lights began to come on and the light shone through her eyelids, she opened them to watch the water cascading into the pool.

Momentarily Ben came walking into her view, her heart flipped and she smiled. He smiled back and beckoned her towards the fountain. She got up and approached him, he put his finger to his lips as if to silence her, she thought it odd but followed his direction. When she was close enough he reached out and placed his hand on her upper arm, as he had done earlier in the day. His firm hand on her arm felt comforting and she felt solace in his touch.

"Hi" he said kindly, just loud enough to be heard over the noisy water "Let's sit down"

He steered her towards the edge of the fountain and they sat down, his hand still on her arm. The closer they were to the fountain, the noisier it was and it was cooler sat there with the mist from the water. She wasn't about to complain but she did find it slightly odd when there were so many benches free that he could have picked, including the one she had been sat on.

"Ms. Sinclair, I'm so glad I found you, I have a lot to tell you. I know you must have a lot of questions."

"I do, although first off, please call me Purdy" she felt crestfallen that he didn't use her first name, it felt so impersonal.

"Of course, Purdy," he said smiling "It's a good name!" she blushed.

"Thanks… I don't know where to start…" she began.

"No need" he stopped her "Let me start, and to begin with there are a few things that you *have* to know. And its going to be difficult for you to comprehend, I think, but I'm going to try to help you, ok?" she nodded, and felt a mixture of dread, curiosity and excitement all at once, what did this cute stranger in this odd place have to tell her and why did he wish to help her?

"OK, here goes. First of all, you are probably wondering why I keep grabbing your arm when we meet," of all the things he could have started with, no this was not the most pressing, she liked his touch and the idea that it was for a reason other than he fancied her was a little disappointing "You've have a small microchip embedded in your arm…"

"No I haven't!" Purdy was indignant, she'd been very adamant not to sign up to any microchipping which was why people rolled their eyes when she pulled her phone out to make payments, she was in quite the minority in that respect, she tried to pull herself free but Ben's grip got firmer on her arm.

"Purdy, I'm sorry, but you *have* been microchipped although it was without your consent, please wait I need to tell you the whole story" he implored her, she relaxed a little and his grip loosened "Do you remember recently having a medical which involved a tetanus shot?" she nodded as she recalled the impromptu medical she had been called for and the unusually painful shot she'd received. "It wasn't a tetanus shot, it was a small microchip which tracks everything about you. It tracks your location, it hears everything you say and it links to all records ever made of and by you, including your entire internet history, your banking, your likes, your dislikes, everything you have ever bought, read, written, everything is tracked back to that chip."

Purdy's mind was reeling, she'd been chipped without her knowing? It felt like such a violation, she felt a little sick and her first thought was to get rid of it, she tried again to pull away from Ben's grip but he held on to her tightly.

"Purdy, you have to stop, the only way we can talk like this now is because I'm holding your arm where the chip is. I have a piece of copper in my hand which is helping somewhat to block the signal, and along with the noise from the fountain, it's helping to hinder them from eavesdropping our conversation. Do you understand?"

Purdy's eyes began to well up, she felt overwhelmed by all of this "How do I get rid of it?" she asked him quietly, fighting back the tears.

"Right now, you can't, you have to keep it" a tear escaped and trickled down her face, this wasn't what she had wanted to hear "But that's only for now, I will help you remove it when the time is right, I promise. OK?"

"OK but when will the time be right? What is happening, Ben?"

"The time will be right when we escape from here." Escape? The word echoed in her head, why would they escape, they would be let out of here as soon as their quarantine was over so why the need to be so dramatic about escaping?

"What? What are you talking about Ben, who are you and what are you doing here?" she was suddenly suspicious of this stranger trying to tell her crazy things.

"Those are fair questions and you have every right to be suspicious of me" he began "I'm not a mechanic, that's the only untruthful thing I've ever led you to believe about me. My name *is* Ben and I *am* here to help you. I'm a member of a Resistance group. We became concerned about people disappearing and have been investigating how and why it is happening."

Resistance, she thought to herself, what is this? World War Two France? People disappearing, microchips and escapes, this was all a little much for a corporate lawyer from a small English town, how on earth did she get messed up with all this? Maybe it was a dream, she poked herself in the leg, it didn't wake her, she continued listening to Ben's story.

"About seven years ago people started going missing. At first it was people who no one would notice were missing. Homeless people and transients were rounded up and removed from the streets. Nobody really paid attention, most were pleased that the streets seemed to get cleaned up. Prisoners who were held in federal institutions who had no friends or family on the outside also started to disappear, as did the disabled and sick, officials claimed they had been transported to other facilities, which wasn't entirely untrue. They were brought places like this."

"They needed quarantining too?" Purdy was slow on the uptake and realized what she said as soon as it left her mouth.

"This isn't a quarantine facility," Ben said gently "There's nothing wrong with you, they have other plans for you which is why you are here."

"Other plans?"

"Yes, I'll get to that in a little while. For now, you need to know all the background. I know this is frustrating and confusing for you but please do bear with me. Where was I? Oh yes, so all these people were moved to camps like this. It was considered a good way to clean up the streets and as the people that were moved were generally loners or the unloved, nobody was there to make a fuss so it just happened with either no one noticing or if they did notice, doing nothing about it."

Purdy took this in, she considered the last few years and he was right, there were no longer homeless people on the streets of San Francisco like there once had been. And crime rates were down, as all articles seemed to report. She'd not put a lot of thought into how or why this had happened she, and she assumed everyone else, was just happy with the safety and pleasantness of this 'cleaned up' world that they saw no need to question it. However now it dawned on her that what Ben was saying may well be true, things had changed significantly in the last few years, it didn't, however explain how she came to be here.

"So this went on for a couple of years," he continued on "when they took the people they sorted them into groups. Either they were considered useless and were immediately disposed of or they were taken to the rehabilitation clinics to be cleaned up and then deposited in places like the one we're in now for future use."

"Oh that's awful! Disposed of?! Like unwanted animals at the shelter?" Purdy exclaimed "And what 'future use', I don't understand, who are 'they'? The government? What happens after here?"

Ben held up his other hand, the one that wasn't holding Purdy's arm.

"I'm getting to all of that, hold up a sec. I'm sorry I know there's a lot you want to know but I have to tell you it in a logical way so you get the full picture." Purdy nodded, her head was spinning with so many questions but he couldn't answer them all at once she held her tongue and let him continue on.

"After the first couple of years they realized that they had managed to dispose of what they considered the bad elements and they could expand their plans. They could use these facilities for dark purposes and they started to broaden their reach. Purdy, these facilities, they are referred to as population reduction centers." he paused, he knew that this would be hard to take in for her and he could see she was already struggling to comprehend all of this. She sat there dumbfounded staring at him, considering the term 'population reduction'.

"In order to help them track people and to monitor the population for the people who should be reduced and the people who should be kept they started microchipping people at every opportunity. First they started off by using medical practitioners to tell all patients who visited that they required a shot of some description, sometimes it was a tetanus, other times it was a flu shot. Soon enough a large proportion of the population had been chipped. Medical records and credit card details were used to collate files on every person. The chip feeds back information on health, whereabouts, social media, political affiliations, and obviously it can hear every tiny detail about the individual which all gets collected in one place, by one organization, who can pinpoint their whereabouts at any second of any day."

Purdy was speechless, she was trying to take it all in, but population reduction presumably didn't mean reducing the obesity epidemic, it meant reducing the amount of people in the population. She was here to be reduced? In other words, she was surplus to requirements? But whose requirements? She was still confused about who this organization could be and how they could get away with doing this.

"So... Population reduction...?" she didn't even know how to ask the question really, Ben hung his head and then looked her directly in the eyes.

"Yes." he said. "It is exactly what it sounds like... it is a way to reduce the amount of people in the population. Based on the decisions of just a few, as to who they deem to be worthy of living and who is not."

"Who? Who is deciding that?!" Purdy was outraged, Ben shook his head.

"I can't give you a definitive answer on that, it's something we're still investigating. Do you remember about five years ago there was a crazy Black Friday sale at all Allmart stores?" She nodded, it had been big news, she remembered. "This was a huge push to get more people chipped. In order to take advantage of the crazy deals they were offering customers had to agree to payment by embedded chip. Most people just blindly agreed and had chips implanted in them as it was suggested to them that chip payment would be the way of the future anyway, they may as well get in early and take advantage of the sale."

"I remember that!" it came back to Purdy in a flash, it had been on the news that no one had been informed of this before they got to the stores and some people had been furious and made a huge fuss about it (rightly so, she thought, you must be mad to allow a store to microchip you like a pet) and others just shrugged and allowed the chipping to happen as they couldn't pass up the bargains on offer.

"Clearly, the chips are not just used for payment. They use them to find out who are the easiest people to take. The people who won't be missed. People who don't have many family ties, or people who they consider to have questionable morals who they will be able to use internet use against in order to create viable stories as to why someone has disappeared if anyone should raise suspicion with officials."

And Purdy herself had one of these chips now, she felt so violated, completely without privacy, she was horrified. But why her? She didn't feel she had questionable morals. She also hoped that people would notice if she was missing, but it was true she had no family here, just friends and Fred appeared to have all but given up on her, she felt sad and hopeless, maybe they were right to have taken her.

"Now this is going to be hard to hear, but you need the full picture," Ben took a deep breath "Future uses vary. You see how people in this place are separated into three different houses, wearing three different colors of clothes? You are blue, blue means you're in holding, they have a use for you but that use hasn't become necessary yet. From blue you either become black or red. You may have noticed that women in black are all pregnant? That is their first purpose. They may then return to blue, become red or be disposed of, depending on temperament and usefulness."

"Wait, have I been brought here to breed?" Purdy was horrified, this all seemed so inhuman.

Ben paused, trying to find the right words "No" he said slowly, "Purdy I don't wish to offend you but you are too old for breeding purposes here in The Facility."

Purdy was both relieved and insulted, too old?! She wasn't even 40 yet.

"They only breed women who are between the ages of 16 and 26."

"16 and 26? But some of those 'women' are still pretty much children, what the hell is this all about? I know, I know you're getting to it but Ben, seriously, what the fuck?"

"Its ok, I get it, I've had a couple of years to learn all this and process it, I'm throwing it all at you in one go, it's hard to comprehend. I really can't get into what the babies are eventually used for as its just too horrifying." Ben stopped momentarily to collect his thoughts, Purdy's mind was whirring over what they would do to the poor babies and the 'disposable' mothers, waves of nausea swept through her. "and for you personally I haven't even got to the worst of it." he continued "I have to prepare you for what happens once you move into the red house."

She'd not spent much time thinking about the red house, it didn't occur to her that a whole other group of people lived in there as she didn't see many people in red. And the few she did see were in the gym where she'd assumed that was just a different outfit for trainers to wear.

"The purpose for a lot of the people in blue, you included, Purdy, is because you are a perfect match for some wealthy person's donor needs. The red house is used for harvesting organs. The wealthy pay vast sums of money for people who turn out to be a match for them to be kept healthy and in comfort here until they require them. Other people in blue, who don't have a specific donee that they belong to, will be used for human experimentation, used like lab rats. Once they have fulfilled that purpose, they are finally disposed of, no one ever leaves here... well not alive anyway." Ben stopped to allow Purdy to process what he'd just told her

Purdy thought she was going to vomit, she contemplated the things that Ben was telling her. How could any of this be possible? Who sanctioned such a place? How do you get away with it without people knowing? She looked at him, wondering if he was telling her the truth. What had he to gain in telling her lies? What could he want from her? She'd only met him once before this and surely he couldn't have hunted her down just because she suggested he'd recorded a video of her, could he?

"Wait, how do you know all of this? And why did you come looking specifically for me? We only met once, you barely know me"

"I had to," Ben hung his head "Purdy I feel terrible, it's my fault that you're here."

Reeling from revelations

"What do you mean, it's your fault?" Purdy was reeling from all the information that she had just been given, she could barely take it all in. "We've only met once, how can I be here, how can my life be hanging by a thread, because of you?"

"The red light on the tablet that you pointed out? I didn't know..."

"Wait... you mean when I accused you of recording me? You mean you were? What the... you made me feel terrible about that, like I was a lunatic for suggesting it and you were recording me the whole time?! Why?" she exploded at him.

"Shh, we don't want to be heard over the fountain, please calm down, let's not arouse any suspicion we need to keep inconspicuous." Ben implored her "No, I didn't record you and I had no idea it was happening. The company that I was working for, that I had infiltrated in order to investigate the disappearance of some people, used the tablets to scan people to check for microchips. When I was inputting details the tablet scanned you, that was the red light. The scan showed that you didn't have a chip and it flagged you immediately in the system."

Purdy considered this, indeed the medical requirement had appeared in her inbox within minutes of her meeting with Ben that same day. Oh dear god, had she just ignored the request for a medical she might not be here? But she couldn't have done that, it was a governmental requirement, or at least she thought it was. Was the government behind this?

"I didn't know, I swear I didn't know. I've taken that tablet out many times and it must have scanned many people, some of whom may also not have been chipped but just by meeting me they were likely flagged and chipped too. I didn't know that I was assisting the system which I thought I was helping to bring down. I only found out after you made a fuss and I looked into the red light issue. I hacked into the computer system and I found your file, I found out that you were taken that night and brought here."

"But I don't understand. You work for them? How did you get in here then? I'll be honest, Ben, I want to believe you but right now you're looking a bit dodgy to me."

"I can understand that and I don't blame you. Look I want to get you out of this, since my resistance group have been involved we've managed to assist some people to escape. I requested that I be allowed to come and help you personally as I feel responsible for you. I have a fake chip in my arm, my group can manipulate it with their own technology, I managed to get brought here to find you and assist your escape."

It sounded viable to Purdy, considering all the other strange things that had happened recently, she thought about her options and in reality, if what Ben was telling her was all true then she needed him and she was prepared to believe him in order to get out of here. Her memory and thoughts had been so cloudy recently but right now things seemed so clear to her, she had to escape and she had to do it soon.

"OK, so suppose I do believe you and I'm willing to work with you, what is it that I need to do, when can we go? Can we go tonight?"

Ben relaxed a little, relieved that Purdy was willing not to just write him off as a nut job.

"Sorry, tonight isn't possible, but tomorrow we have a chance, there's an escape attempt fixed for tomorrow evening, do you want to attempt it?"

Purdy nodded, she did, more than anything she wanted to escape and regain some normality.

"OK good" Ben raised a small smile "There's just some things you need to do, OK? First off, the food situation"

"Oh yeh I stuck to the carbs and milk thing this morning but by the evening I'd forgotten what you said, I don't know why but my memory has been shocking recently but I'm feeling more clarity now than I have in a while."

"It's the food. The food is drugged with compounds which make you forget things and leave most people with a sense of euphoria, it's to keep the inmates sedate and compliant. Have you noticed how it is some of the best tasting food you've ever had?"

"Yes!"

"Yep, that's to encourage you to eat it all, so you get the maximum dose. What did you have for dinner? Whatever it was seems to have helped because you're more lucid than a lot of others."

"I had pasta in a creamy sauce, it's not a dish I would normally order funnily enough but Jenny ordered it and it sounded good so I ordered it too, maybe your carbs advice resonated with me even though I forgot?"

"Maybe..."

"It caused a right old fuss actually" Purdy continued "When it arrived Jenny wanted the one I picked up but I wouldn't let her have it, they were identical, I don't know why she was being so weird about it."

"Who's Jenny?" Ben enquired.

"She's, uh, a friend... well friend might be overstating it actually, she's the first person I met when I came here, she kind of took me under her wing, told me the rules and introduced me to others..." she tailed off as she saw Ben's expression change. "Ben? Are you ok?"

"Yeh... you didn't tell Jenny that you were meeting me did you?" he was concerned.

"No, I didn't tell anyone. Why, what's wrong?"

"There are some inmates in the blue house who are there voluntarily. They aren't being drugged, they were offered a deal, they work for The Facility, assisting in keeping inmates under control in exchange for a relative life of luxury to the one they experienced before coming here. The inmates are monitored by their chips, by the drones and by other cameras hidden around the place. The problem is that the technology isn't exactly infallible. Just like I can trick your chip with my copper, water can hinder communications too, hence why I suggest we meet by the fountain. Not only does noise help cover us while we talk, the water interferes somewhat with signals. The people are added as a set of eyes on the ground. They live amongst us and if they see any sign of trouble, like you making friends with me for example, they report it and The Facility can deal with it."

Purdy's blood ran cold. She never trusted Jenny, it wouldn't surprise her if she was in on things, it would explain her rule obsession.

"It's possible that Jenny works here and has been assigned to you. The plates of food may have looked identical to you but there is likely some sign for her to show what is drugged and what is not so she doesn't get the wrong meals."

"That would explain why she didn't eat her's, she just pushed it around the plate."

"Well I can't say for certain, but we should be wary of her at least. Here" Ben was handing Purdy a small bag of small red tablets that looked a bit like Advil,. "Take one of these before each meal, they should neutralize the compound and leave you clear headed. You also will avoid raising suspicion as you continue to eat normally. Keep them in your pocket and don't take them out anywhere other than your bathroom. Your bathroom is the only place without cameras, they can't track what you do in there, other than if they can hear you through your chip."

Purdy nodded, it felt odd to be accepting pills from a virtual stranger and just trust that she should take them but this is what her life had become it seemed. She put them in her pocket.

"And it goes without saying, not to mention our meeting or knowing each other to anyone else. If you happen to see me outside of times we've arranged to meet, ignore me, as I will you."

"Got it. So what's the plan for tomorrow evening" Purdy was anxious to get started on her escape, as the drugs wore off she felt more and more desperate to separate herself from this place and these people, all of whom she was wary of trusting.

"OK, so after dark it is possible to move undetected to a part of the boundary where you can cross and make it to safety. It's about a two mile walk to get to the boundary, are you up for that?"

"Of course, but where, which direction?" Purdy suddenly realized that she had not in fact left the square since arriving here in the dead of night, she had no idea what was down the roads which led between the buildings and, until now, she'd had no interest in learning either. Boy, those drugs were powerful.

"You take the road which goes between the blue house and the red house. It's important to wait until after dark and to stick close to the building so as not to be seen leaving the square. Here, take this." He handed her a small metallic square. "It has an adhesive backing on it. Just before you leave your room, put it over where your chip is on your arm, it will temporarily hinder the signal whilst you're moving, they won't be able to track where you are easily."

Purdy took the square patch from him and put it in her pocket with the pills.

"So, you take that road and keep walking for about 2 miles, it turns into a track between the trees so as long as stay on it, walking straight with trees on either side of you you're going the right way. Stick to the edge of the road, the darkness and the trees will hide you from sight and your patch will hide your chip from being monitored. And as long as no one sees you leave, you should be able to stay unnoticed until you reach the fence. A team of people from the resistance will be there waiting for you, they have a 30 minute window between 9.30 and 10pm where they can scramble the signals from the sensors on the fence without being discovered. It's important that you are at the fence by 10pm, otherwise they will have to leave without you."

"Aren't you coming too?"

"We can't leave the square at the same time, we would be easier to detect but I'll meet you at the fence. Unless something goes wrong and I can't turn back I won't be leaving though, I still have work to do in here. Don't worry, my team will take care of you and get you to safety. Their plan will be to get you to the British Consulate General in San Francisco, do you know where that is?"

"No, I didn't even know there was a Consulate here!" Purdy felt a little foolish, surely in the time she had been here she'd have thought at least once about where she would go in an emergency? But the reality was, until recently she'd had no need to be concerned for her own safety, or so she had believed.

"Yes, it's on Sansome Street, number 1 Sansome Street, got it?"

"Yup" 1 Sansome Street, there was no way she was going to allow herself to forget that, the British government had to take care of her, right? She was a British citizen after all!

"So it will probably take you about 40 minutes to walk there in the dark, make sure you leave the square by 9.15 at the latest just to be on the safe side. Sunset is supposed to be at 7.36pm tomorrow so this should give you ample time between then to leave and get yourself to the designated spot."

Purdy nodded her agreement.

"Oh and the last thing, I know now that your memory is coming back it will be tempting to use your phone to contact your friends and tell them what's going on. Don't. The Facility monitors all incoming and outgoing messages as it runs the network that the phones are connected to, there's no way to bypass it. It either stops the messages from coming and going or it changes the content of them so people on the outside don't learn the truth and people on the inside don't remember that people outside will be missing them."

Purdy took all this in, she could only hope that this was the reason why Fred had been so un-Fred-like in recent messages, because they weren't his messages at all, he probably did still care about her. Maybe he was frantic? She couldn't wait to get to the other side of the fence so she could speak to him again.

"So, that's about it" Ben concluded, he smiled at Purdy "I know, this is so much to take in. You've taken it all on board really well though, so I have high hopes that this time tomorrow we will be well on our way to making this just a horrible memory. You ok? Any questions?"

Purdy thought for a moment.

"No, no questions. I think I'm ok. This is all a bit of a shock but I appreciate that you've risked your own safety to come and help me."

"Of course, right well, until tomorrow at the fence then," Ben gave her arm a gentle squeeze and then let go and began to walk away. Purdy sat their motionless for a moment, taking it all in, thinking about all she'd just been told. Ben turned around and gave her one last smile, he mouthed "good luck!" to her and he was gone off into the darkness.

Purdy walked back to her room mulling it all over, annoyed and upset that anyone felt they had the right to do this to her. She still didn't know who exactly was behind all this, but she felt damn sure she planned to find out and shout it from the rooftops once she was out of there.

The longest day

Purdy had a terrible night's sleep. The worst since she had arrived here, likely it was partly to do with the drugs wearing off but she also had so many new things swimming around her head it was hard to stop her mind from whirring and she tossed and turned for hours. Who the hell were these people who got to play at being Gods and decide who lives and who dies? Or who is not worthy of a life of their own and is only of use if they can donate their organs to another or be experimented on? The people who are allowed to live, to thrive, are able to *just* because they are wealthy? *Just* because they have more in the bank, more property, more land, how did that make them more worthy? How did it make them better people? She considered this, and it was true, as far back as she could recall from the history she was aware of, this really had always been the way, the wealthy control the poor, the haves control the have-nots, the most aggressive defeat the more meek, it felt so unfair and unbalanced to her.

It was also unbelievable to her mind that in this so overtly connected world, where every other person posted every plate of food that they ever ate or every selfie that they took all day everyday for the rest of the world to see, how could this happen without anyone noticing, without anyone drawing attention to it? Had the human race really become so self-obsessed and narcissistic now that they could care less that these things went on? Striving for themselves to join the ranks of the super wealthy, blissfully ignorant of the fate that might await them if they posted something on line which was frowned upon by those few wealthy or if it just turned out that they happened to share the same tissue type of the child or significant other of a person who happened to have vast sums of wealth who could buy an unsuspecting donor to fix their own problem.

She was overwhelmed with grief for it all and felt the danger she was in of slipping into depression, struggling to process the enormity of it all. In a bid to take her mind off of it until she had more head space to contemplate it she made plans to work on her escape when she could push the horrors from her consciousness. She had made a mental note of all of Ben's instructions, and decided that she would leave her room as soon as the sun set and it was dark outside to make her way to the fence as early as possible, there was no way she was going to miss this chance to escape from this living morgue.

She'd eventually fallen asleep in the early hours of the morning so when the daylight streamed in through the window it took a while to rouse her. Once awake everything, the full horror of where she was and her predicament washed over her like a wave of despair. She pushed it to the back of her mind. There was no point dwelling on it, she only needed to get through today.

Having somewhat lost her appetite and with her newfound disgust for Jenny she was reluctant to go over and meet the others for breakfast that morning. But heeding Ben's warning about keeping things to herself she thought it best to keep carrying on as if today was the same as yesterday had been. She forced herself out of bed and into the bathroom to get ready. Just before she was ready to leave she popped one of the red pills into her mouth and swallowed, there was no way she was going to let that drugged food turn off her senses again.

She joined the others for breakfast as usual, she sat down and looked at them all. Jenny looked her usual smug, self satisfied self, Purdy grimaced in an attempt to be cordial to her, and then reminded herself that she must stay undetected. She approached them all with a breezy nonchalance and ordered from the tablet as usual, reverting to her normal breakfast of egg white omelette. She couldn't be sure but she thought she saw a glimmer of approval on Jenny's face at her choice and felt pleased that she could might just pull off this ruse after all.

They chatted away as normal but she noticed a difference with the demeanor of Georgia and Derek, they seemed slower to her, a bit like if they were slightly stoned. She realized that they were likely always like this due to the the effect of the drugs and it was she who was being closer to her normal self today, rather than the two of them actually being slower so she proceeded to attempt to mimic them to add further weight to her pretense, if she seemed too alert this might tip Jenny off to her and she could do without Jenny sniffing around her today.

When her food arrived she ate it in silence, listening to the others chatter and closely monitoring every bite to see whether she felt any change to her mental alertness. Gladly there seemed to be no effect that she could detect but the ordinarily delicious food now was a chore to eat due to her knowledge of what it was laced with.

"Are you going for a swim today?" Jenny's question broke into Purdy's thoughts.

"Huh, oh yeh... as usual" Purdy thought it was odd of her to ask but maybe she was being paranoid, Jenny was probably just making conversation after the awkwardness of yesterday. "Oh, hey how did your VRing go last night? Did you steal any potions or gold?"

"Yeh it was fun, I finished really late, did you enjoy your walk around the square?" Purdy nodded and took another bite of omelette, she wanted to end the conversation there in case of any further prying, she held her breath in case Jenny had seen her talking to Ben and was about to pry into it. Thankfully Jenny turned her attentions to Derek and was asking him about how the play was going.

If anyone had happened to see her talking to Ben she needed a cover story but what was her excuse, she racked her brains and then settled on the idea that she would just say he had approached her to ask about where he could get gym clothes, just like that first conversation she had with Chuck... Chuck! It came back to Purdy in a wave of sadness, she'd seen Chuck only yesterday in the gym, wearing red, Chuck had become a donor. Oh poor, friendly Chuck, what could she do? Could she help him? Her mind was frantic but she had to try and appear like nothing was wrong to the others. She finished her last bite and put down her fork.

"Hey sorry I'm going to dash off, want to get to the pool!" she stood up, the others looked surprised at her keenness to get off, ordinarily Purdy was the last to leave the table, she thought quickly "need the loo too", she winked and hated herself immediately, seriously was using the toilet the only excuse she could come up with under pressure? She needed to work on that.

She made her way quickly back to her room thinking about Chuck all the way. Having not noticed him since that first day she had met him, she wondered when he had moved to the red clothing, had he already been used as a donor? Surely not, he hadn't looked cheerful as such yesterday, but he also didn't look like someone who had so much as donated blood, let alone another vital organ.

Grabbing her swimsuit and towel she headed over to the gym, if Chuck was there she would definitely go over and speak to him today, unclear of what she would actually say she hoped it would come to her in the moment. Could she tell him she knew his fate? No, she didn't feel she could do that, in fact it would be hard for her to tell him anything at all, they were both chipped after all. She felt despondent but hoped for a miracle.

When she walked in through the gym door she looked around. It was pretty busy in there, she noticed that no one looked especially happy, they seemed, on the whole, to all be quite zombie-like, just staring at screens or off into the distance. She'd not seen this before, the drugged food had obviously had the effect of making others seem different than they actually are, or it just completely numbed the taker to the reality around them and they created their own version in their head. Her eyes searched the room, trying to pick out the people in red trying to see Chuck's face. Nothing, she sighed, there was no sign of Chuck, she'd check again after her swim.

The pool didn't look as idyllic today. It was still a magnificent size and she had a lane to herself so it was still beating a lot of other public pools she'd been too but the water didn't look as inviting as it had done before today. Having a swim alone was still preferable to hitting the treadmill surrounded by those poor zombies though so she dived in anyway, she needed the distraction, the wait for sunset was unbearable.

After her swim she walked back through the gym, searching for Chuck, still no sign of him. She felt an awful sense of doom, maybe no one outside of the red building would ever see Chuck again. Poor Chuck, she wished she'd been more friendly to him on that first day now.

At lunchtime she went over to meet the others, but not without taking a red pill first. She started to find the company of her fellow inmates quite excruciating, and this just made the time drag on even longer. Again she made great strives to hope that Jenny didn't notice any difference in her demeanor, and again she listened to them drone on about nothing of substance. Knowing the 'rules' meant they couldn't talk about their lives outside of The Facility made for extremely dull conversations about the same old things. Again her food was not as delicious and she navigated a not so riveting conversation about a tv show that the other three appeared to have recently discovered and all were watching. She promised faithfully to take a look for herself soon so she could join in whilst secretly telling herself not to worry this would all be over soon enough.

In the afternoon she went back to her room and made plans. In order not to draw negative attention to herself when she was leaving that evening she chose not to take her handbag with her, she picked it up and took it into the bathroom with her. If she was going to go through it she wanted do that alone without being monitored, the last bastion of privacy she had left. She upended it on the bathroom floor and studied the contents, deciding what she could take in her pockets and what she could leave behind, never to see again. Things she would definitely take included her phone, passport, wallet and a lip balm. Things she could live without included her emergency make up touch up kit, her hair brush and actual Advil, she didn't want to mix them up with her pills that Ben had given her. She filled her pockets in readiness for the evening.

She hung her bag back on the chair, where it would remain after she left. It was a shame, she really liked that bag, it was practical but needs must. She then called up a movie to watch, wanting something to give her courage she considered asking for The Great Escape but fearing that was too much on the nose she went for some crappy romantic comedy instead and used the time to take a little nap.

When she awoke it was already dinner time. She had no appetite but once again felt she must go and put on a show for Jenny at least. She took another of her red pills in the bathroom and started off across the square to the Cafe.

In order to give her the energy for the two mile walk in the dark to the fence later that evening Purdy decided to order banana pancakes with a side of bacon for dinner. Jenny eyed it up when it arrived.

"Hungry?" she asked Purdy

"Famished" Purdy said with a smile "had a long hard swim today, it left me ravenous!"

"I thought that was this morning, did you go again this afternoon?"

"What? Uh, no, in fact this afternoon I just hung out but the swim this morning really took it out of me." Purdy was irritated by Jenny's prying but tried to sound breezy in her replies, just this one last meal to get through after all.

"Oh right," Jenny eyed her suspiciously, it seemed strange to her that Purdy would be ordering something so densely packed with calories just before bedtime. "Well, if you feel full and want to work that off this evening I'm off to do some more of my VRing game, you could come with me this time?"

"oh... thanks" Purdy choked down her bite of pancake, she was running out of excuses with Jenny but she certainly was not going to sign up for VRing tonight, she was glad to hear though that Jenny would be distracted so unable to spy on Purdy "but that swim really wiped me out, thought I'd have an early night tonight."

"Oh shame, well if you change your mind just let me know, I can add more people to my game."

"I might come" Georgia joined in and on receiving no reply continued "That's if you were inviting me too?"

Jenny paused, looking at Purdy, Purdy shifted uncomfortably in her seat and took another bite of pancake trying to look as though these were the greatest pancakes she'd ever tasted.

"Sure," Jenny was still staring at Purdy "that's settled then its a girls night out, you, me and Georgia, you have to come now, Purdy."

"Oooh girls' night, whoop!" Georgia squealed.

"Not that I'm offended or anything..." chipped in Derek.

"You could come too!" Georgia gave him playful jab in the arm.

"Apparently you have all forgotten that I am being a fabulous actooor still this week, no, no you all go and enjoy your VRing, I must tread the boards!" Derek replied with his trademark flourish.

"Well that's a plan then" Jenny looked satisfied with herself, Purdy was still frantically searching for reasons she couldn't go.

"You know, I am super tired, I don't think I'll be any good at playing tonight and I'll ruin it for us all" she managed to muster.

"Oh pish posh!" unfortunately Georgia had become over enthused about the idea now and although

Purdy may have put Jenny off, Georgia was just impossible to say no to. "We'll have fun, regardless of if we win or not!"

Purdy managed a small smile and a nod. Shit! Now she had to find a way out of this.

Time for some quick thinking

Back in her room Purdy sat on her bed thinking of escape plans. As long as she left before 9.15 she would make it, in fact if worst came to worst and she couldn't leave until 9.30 she would run to make it, she couldn't miss this chance, she just had to find a way to put Jenny and Georgia off. She had considered just not turning up for the VRing but she feared that if Jenny was working for The Facility as she assumed that she was then Jenny would raise an alarm and get both her and Ben in trouble, and even possibly the resistance group, she couldn't chance it.

The best chance she saw for herself was going along to the VRing and then feigning illness around 8.30. That would give her time to leave there, get back to her room, cover her chip and leave again by 9pm. Plenty of time, she started to relax about things, still to be on the safe side she decided to take everything in her pockets that she wanted to leave with just in case she had no time to return to her room before leaving.

She was getting ready to leave and there was a knock at her door. She went over and opened it, Jenny was stood there looking all pleased with herself.

"Hi! Just thought I'd grab you on my way past, no point in us walking over separately as we're going the same place!" Purdy wanted to roll her eyes but stopped herself in time and forced a smile instead.

"Great, great, well I'm ready!" She couldn't run the risk of Jenny wanting to come in and wait so she had to leave without checking she had everything. She closed the door behind them and checked her pockets, it seemed everything was in order, she breathed a sigh of relief and followed Jenny down the hallway.

They met Georgia at the front door and the three of them trekked over to the Gym together. Georgia was very excited and chattered all the way there about how she couldn't wait to give the fantasy game a go, Purdy tried to agree with faux enthusiasm.

They got into the VRing studio and it suddenly occurred to Purdy that there wasn't a clock in there. She wasn't wearing a watch and the only way to know the time was to check her phone. Something people do in the real world without anyone paying any attention but in here no one ever used their phones. She considered her options. While the others were grabbing their VR helmets and gloves she turned and took a quick look at the time on her phone, it was 7.20. She was going to have to try and guess at the time. She'd keep going in the game for what she felt was an hour and then she would feign the illness. She thought claiming a headache would be the best way out. They began the game.

As she was well aware already these fantasy games were not her thing at all, they spent a while getting used to the rules, and what abilities their individual characters had. Jenny, not surprisingly, took the role of team lead. Georgia was an athletic warrior, which suited her and Purdy was a more sedate healer. She had healing abilities in case anyone was to get wounded. She found this a little passive and boring but at least she might be able to leave the other two to it and not ruin their game when the time felt right.

After a while of trudging around in the game Purdy felt the time was right to put her plan into action.

"Hey guys. I'm not feeling too good, I'm going to go lie down, enjoy the rest of the game without me" she said just as she was about to take her helmet off.

"Wait!" Jenny turned around and saw Purdy had disengaged, she took her helmet off too. "What's wrong?"

"Oh just a bit of headache and wearing the helmet is making me feel worse, I'm just going to go lie down, you stay here, I don't want to ruin the night for us all." Purdy silently urged Jenny to just leave her alone.

Georgia was still in the game, it made Purdy smirk to see her walking around in her helmet and gloves, waving at nothing. Jenny had taken off her helmet completely now.

"No, I'm not leaving you to go back alone if you feel unwell, I'm coming with you." She slipped her helmet back on to tell Georgia it was time to leave. Purdy contemplated making a run for it, she quickly looked at her phone, 8.30 phew, she still had time to get out of here and ditch Jenny, she just needed to keep her cool.

Jenny and Georgia took off their helmets.

"Ah that's a shame, Purd, well we can always come back tomorrow!" Georgia said as she removed her gloves. Purdy smiled slightly, whilst thinking that she really hoped not.

The three of them walked back to the Blue Mansion together, Georgia parted ways with them at the door and went to her corridor, Purdy and Jenny walked to Purdy's door together.

"Why don't I come in with you and make sure you're ok" Jenny pushed herself into the room, looking around. Luckily Purdy had left nothing incriminating on display in there but she certainly didn't want Jenny snooping into her bathroom where her notebook had been left.

"NO!" Purdy said, a little more firmly than she intended "No, thank you Jenny, I really just need to lie down in peace on my own. I appreciate your concern though, you really are a good friend."

She sickened herself with her lies but it was the only way to deal with it.

"Hmm, well ok but if you need anything you give me a shout, ok?" Jenny said brightly as Purdy physically shuffled her out of the door again.

"I will, thanks again! Good night!" Purdy closed the door quickly and leant back onto it listening to Jenny leaving. She heard her footsteps walking away and breathed out another sigh of relief.

Purdy walked into the bathroom and sat on the lid of the toilet seat. She pulled her phone out of her pocket, 8.50 now, she'd give it 10 minutes and then make her way outside again. She sat there checking all the other things in her pockets, she had the lip balm and her wallet, she opened her wallet and found some dollars inside as well as her cards. She was glad to have the dollars, she felt it would be unwise to use her cards if they were all linked to her chip. She hoped someone at the Consulate would help sort all this out so she could go back to her own life, maybe then the cards would be usable again.

She found the copper patch that Ben had given her to put over her chip. She waited until the very last moment to put it on, peeling off the back and carefully placing it squarely over where she could feel the lump of the chip. Putting everything back in her pockets she went over to the door and carefully opened it, hoping beyond hope that nobody else would be out in the hallway.

Opening the door slowly, she peeked out, no sign of anyone yet, she opened the door a little wider, holding her breath, she stepped into the hallway. As she closed the door quietly behind her she was suddenly aware of a buzzing noise, oh crap, was it a drone? To be on the safe side she opened the door and stepped back inside again, closing it behind her and listening for the drone to pass. It passed her door and she heard it go down the hallway and into someone's room. She waited a minute or so to hear it come back. The familiar sound passed her door again and she stood there straining to listen to hear anything else. All seemed quiet and she slowly opened the door again.

She closed the door quietly behind her, this time she heard no noise and breathed out slowly.

"Hey! You looking for me?"

Purdy jumped into next week and spun around, bloody Jenny was stood there next to her beaming. Dear god, was this woman a robot? She couldn't shake her.

"Hey, erm no, I was just thinking some fresh air might make me feel better."

"Ah good idea, I'll join you!" Purdy couldn't catch a break.

"I'd rather be alone." She attempted to put her off.

"Nonsense, if you're sick you need support, no arguments I'm coming."

Purdy's shoulders dropped, she really couldn't shake Jenny. She needed to get out of the building without being noticed but she was running out of ideas. The two women walked out of the building together in silence.

"Ooh, chillier out here than I expected!" Purdy said as they stepped out. It wasn't particularly but she was still looking for ways to get rid of Jenny.

"Well let's go back in then."

"Oh I'm ok, just you don't need to be out here too!" she tried.

"I'm not chilly, I was just thinking of you" Jenny persisted.

Silent again, they walked towards the square and sat on a bench. Purdy had run out of ideas, she just did not know what else to do, she hoped for fate to intervene. They sat together watching the fountain. Jenny attempted small talk but Purdy was losing patience and just grunted in response, blaming her headache for her lack of social skills that evening.

Purdy lost track of how long they had been there and had pretty much resigned herself to the fact she'd lost her chance when Jenny suddenly got up.

"Right, I've got chilly now! Are you coming back inside?"

"Hmm, no, I think I'll sit out here a while longer the air is actually helping." Purdy hoped this was her miracle.

"Ok, well don't get too cold! I'll see you tomorrow" and with that Jenny walked off.

Finally, Purdy thought. She gave it until she saw Jenny walk through the front door of the Blue Mansion and she swiftly got off the bench. Making her way towards the path between the Red and Blue buildings. She briefly looked around, thankfully there were no other people around and no sign of any drones. She didn't dare look at her phone to check the time in case the light from the screen would draw unnecessary attention.

When she got to the Blue Mansion she kept close to the building to stay in the shadows as per Ben's instructions. She quietly and quickly followed the road between the buildings. It was a dark night but her eyes adjusted well and she could make out the shapes of trees along the sides and soon got her bearings. The ground wasn't flat, it was hilly but she broke into a jog, not knowing how long she and Jenny had been in the square she didn't want to run the risk of not making it the 2 miles in good time if it was later than she thought.

It was super quiet out here, she felt she should be afraid but the adrenaline and the fear of not making it to the escape point kept her focussed. She'd been jogging for about a mile when she thought she heard a noise behind her. Too terrified to turn she just upped her pace and turned her jog to a run, she had no idea what she was running from but fear took control. She heard the noise again, she thought it might be footsteps, maybe they were her own? She didn't think so and if she could just keep running she must almost be at the fence now.

Running at full speed now, suddenly someone grabbed her around the waist and she lost her footing. As she stumbled she felt a hand come across her mouth to silence her and the pair of them fell to the ground between some trees, in a heap.

Despair

Lying in a crumpled heap on the grass, limbs entangled, Purdy felt dazed but fearful, she struggled to break free from this person's grasp which just got tighter and tighter. She fought to get their hand off her mouth as she gasped for air. If only she could break free she still might make it to the fence.

"Purdy, hey, its me, its Ben, calm down, I'm not trying to hurt you." Ben whispered into her ear.

Ben? Why on earth was he trying to stop her, Purdy relaxed a little and he loosened his grip on her. Removing his hand from her mouth, she gasped for air, breathing heavily from running, and trying to get air into her lungs following the hand restriction on her mouth.

"Ben?" she gasped at him. "Ben, what are you doing? Am I almost there? Where are your friends? Am I too late?"

"Shh" he put his hand up to her mouth again "We're not the only ones out here. Did someone follow you?" she shook her head, she didn't think so, she'd been really careful "Don't make a move until I say."

They laid there in relative silence for a short time. Faintly she could hear the buzz of a drone, her heart sank, surely the drone would find them. Her heart was pounding, Ben moved slightly and covered her completely with his body, the weight of him was comforting but she was too terrified to really enjoy it.

The noise of the drone came closer, Purdy held her breath, wondering what would happen if the drone caught them. What could the drone do? Was it weaponized? Would people come and follow it? She could feel her heart starting to race faster and faster. Ben, who could obviously feel her terror, squeezed her slightly in a bid to provide comfort, it helped a little but she could see no way out.

The buzz of the drone was at its peak, it must have been directly above them but Purdy couldn't see it through Ben. She silently pleaded for it to go away and not notice them, and just as if someone had heard her pleas the noise started to get fainter, like the drone was moving on. Her body began to relax a bit more but Ben squeezed her more tightly, she soon understood why, the noise was returning, this time it sounded like there was more than one drone, shit.

Motionless and playing as if they were dead they lay there in silence, both taking small, almost imperceptible breaths. The drones buzzed around and above them. At one point at least one of them seemed to get really close to them, hovering just above ground level. Luckily the trees provided for certain coverage that the drones couldn't maneuver around properly. Eventually the buzz of both drones quietened significantly, as if they had retreated.

"I think they've gone" whispered Ben after some time. "You ok?"

"Yeh I think so" Purdy breathed out a long sigh and took a deeper breath, mentally checking her body for aches and pains "Nothing broken, what happened? Did we miss our chance?"

"Sadly, yeh." Ben sounded despondent. He gently untangled himself from Purdy and they laid on the ground still close that their arms were pressed together and their faces close.

"When can we try again?" Purdy whispered, she refused to give up hope on the first attempt.

Ben was quiet, Purdy followed his lead in case he was listening for more drones.

"Purdy…" he began quietly, "I'm so sorry, that was our only chance."

Her head swam as she took this in, what? How can that be? How was it their only chance? Before she had the chance to ask Ben spoke again.

"OK, lets not get down about it, we're smart people, we can come up with another way out, I'm sure of it. We can't stay here all night, we have to make our way back towards our rooms before we're missed. I don't think those drones saw us so for now they don't necessarily know that we were the ones trying to escape, c'mon" he got up and held his hand out for Purdy to help her too, she stubbornly refused to get up.

"This can't be it!" she hissed "Your friends must still be out there, surely we can still get to them."

"My friends failed, Purdy, somehow The Facility found out about our plan and my friends were unable to scramble the signal. I've also found it impossible to reach them since it happened. I'm cut off now, any plans we make will have to be just the two of us, without outside help, I'm so sorry, I failed."

Purdy's eyes filled with tears but she tried to gulp them down, this was it, how would they escape now? She was stuck here. She'd never see her friends, her house or even England ever again. Refusing to be beaten though she got up, without the help of Ben. She could take care of this, now she was aware she could do something about it, negotiate with their captors perhaps, whoever they were.

"Fine," she said defiantly "It's fine, you're right, we're smart we can work this out."

Ben tried to raise a smile at her and started to walk back along the track, she followed closely behind, with her head down. They didn't speak for the first ten minutes or so. Listening for the drones, hoping they didn't come back.

"So, there's no way you can contact your friends at all now, then?" Purdy broke the silence with her hushed question. Ben didn't answer immediately.

"Ben?" she urged him

"I'm thinking..." Ben replied quietly "I'll have to work on it, see if I can find a way to contact them. It's just all my communications were knocked off line earlier this evening, maybe it's a glitch. But the same rules still apply, we can't be seen to be friendly to each other out in the open, people can't know we know each other, we might arouse more suspicion."

"OK" Purdy sighed "Ben, I'm scared. I saw a guy I met on my first day here and he was wearing red. Is he a donor now? What if I'm next, what if I'm taken to be a donor too? Is there anyway I can stop it from happening?"

"Not that I know of" he replied glumly "But I'll think about it, maybe there's a way we can put them off, honestly I can't think of one though. You can stay strong, I know you can, tonight you were awesome, we were just really unlucky. "

Purdy walked on in silence, what if she was unlucky again and they came tomorrow for her? She was terrified. They were getting closer to the square.

"Remember to take off the patch from your chip when you get back to your bathroom, and keep it safe in case we need to use it again. And keep taking those pills, don't fall back into the drugged up state you were, you need to keep a clear head."

"Yup got it" Purdy whispered despondently.

He turned to her and saw a tear role down her cheek. He reached out to her and enveloped her in a hug, she hugged him back for a moment and then had to pull away else she was in danger of completely losing her cool and sobbing into his firm chest. They could see the Blue Mansion from where they were now standing.

"Ok, you go first" Ben urged her "I'll wait until I see you go into the door before I make my move. Take care, sleep well."

"Night" she said and moved into the shadow of the building to make her way to the door, never looking back.

Getting back into the building was easy and she made it to her room without bumping into anyone. She sat on the lid of the toilet and sobbed. It felt hopeless, what on earth was she to do now. After she'd cried until she could barely open her eyes anymore and her head was beginning to bang she peeled the patch off of her arm and stuck it to the backing paper that she'd pulled it from earlier. Luckily she still had that in her pocket and hadn't disposed of it, not wishing to leave any evidence be-hind. She crawled into bed and fell into a restless sleep, filled with nightmares and terrors, she feared all hope was lost and was struggling to see any light at the end of that foggy tunnel.

Hopelessness?

Purdy stirred awake. She couldn't face getting out of bed this morning. And why should she? The only things she had to do were eat and swim, she could last quite a long time without doing either of those things, she could just lay in her bed for as long as she could stomach.

She ran over the events of last night in her head. Trying to decide if there had been anything else she could have done to have made it work. She didn't think so, it wasn't her lateness that messed things up. It could well have been Jenny, though, maybe Jenny planned to hold her up and told someone of her suspicions which is why the scrambling didn't work and the drones came out hunting.

She considered her helplessness, maybe she should just stop taking the pills that Ben had given her and she would be in blissful ignorance of her situation once again. This was a horrible plan, that was pretty much giving up on life and however desperate she felt she wasn't ready to give in to that just yet.

A knock at the door interrupted her thoughts. It was bound to be Jenny, she ignored it. The knock came again, she pulled the duvet over her head. Footsteps walked away from her door and she was relieved whoever it was had given up on her. She pressed the green button and requested some water, that crying last night had left her dehydrated. Momentarily a drone arrived with her water.

***

She must have fallen back to sleep as she was now being awoken by more knocking. Bloody Jenny.

"Yeh, what is it?" She shouted grumpily at the door.

"Only me!" Jenny shouted shrilly back at her "I wanted to see how you were feeling, still got your headache? We missed you at breakfast time! Let me in!"

"Go away!" Purdy called back without thinking about who she was talking to. "Yes I still have a headache, I just want to be left alone."

"I want to see with my own eyes that you're ok!" Jenny persisted.

"Jenny I'm in bed because I don't feel well but I'm not dying, just leave me to it, I'll see you later, ok?" Purdy felt pleased with how firm she was being, usually she was such a pushover.

"Well alright but I expect you to come find me if you feel any worse, ok?" Jenny said after a brief pause.

"I will" sighed Purdy "Thank you!"

Silence again. Purdy relaxed back into her duvet, satisfied at having got rid of Jenny, but still angry about her unchanging predicament. I'm not getting up today, she said to herself, fuck 'em all, I hate the lot of them.

***

Later that day Purdy was still laying in her bed, she'd ordered up a tv show and binge watched it whilst falling in and out of sleep. At the end of the seventh episode she decided that she would take a shower, she was making no further plans than just that, she'd take a shower and then see how she felt, maybe she would go grab some dinner a little later, maybe not.

She took her time in the shower enjoying the hot water and afterwards sat on the bed pulling her hairbrush through her wet hair. She put the hairbrush down on the desk next to her phone which was lying there charging. She stared into space, thinking about her predicament, it was quiet, not very much noise coming from anywhere but all of a sudden the hairbrush and phone began to tap, clattering against the desktop and breaking her from her thoughts. The curtains began to sway and the windows rattled in their frames.

It sounded like the soundtrack from Titanic when the ship was beginning to break in two and the furniture began to shift and shake. She'd lived in the Bay Area for long enough now to recognize the signs, she knew what was coming. It was the sound of something thundering toward you, something which can't be held back, something unstoppable.

And there it was, right there, the roll of the earthquake under her feet, it hit hard and shook for a long time, longer than she had ever experienced before and the force was way stronger. She looked above her head, thankfully there was nothing above her that could fall so she laid down and wrapped the duvet around her, planning to just wait it out, hopefully this building had been built to withstand a quake. For a brief nanosecond she wondered if it really would be terrible to go this way, with a building collapsing on her rather than living out her fate here but as quickly as she thought it she dismissed it again, she still had in her a survival instinct which trumped that urge she had felt to give up on life.

For about 45 seconds it felt like someone was at the foot of her bed shaking it violently back and forth, it was an awful feeling of no control, there was nothing she could do to stop this, she just had to wait it out. The 45 seconds may as well have been 45 minutes in her head, it was relentless and it started to make her feel violently sick, like an awful fair-ground ride that she knew wasn't going to stop any-time soon.

When the shaking stopped she lay there waiting for the aftershock, would it be as big? Bigger? Please let it be smaller, she thought to herself. In the outside world she would use the internet at such a time, first of all to make sure it was still working and secondly to check for any tsunami warnings, not that she knew whether they were in a tsunami zone or not here. She'd also look to see what size it was, she was guessing it must be at least a 6 but it was im-possible to tell in reality.

Ordinarily immediately after an earthquake, in the city, you'd hear dogs barking and car alarms going off; out here, wherever The Facility was, it was just eerily quiet. No noise at all, Purdy could hear the blood that was pumping faster and flowing through her head quickly due to her racing heart rate. Her breathing had quickened and her pulse was beating like she'd just finished ten laps of the pool, at speed.

After a while she moved and sat up, nothing yet, no after shock. She wasn't sure if this was a bad sign or a good one. She placed the duvet back on the bed and looked around her room. Luckily there was nothing that could fall or be damaged in there and the building seemed to have held up alright. Maybe, while it was still, she should go outside and see what others were doing, maybe get out of the building just in case it wasn't safe. She got up and went to walk into the bathroom, the aftershock hit, nowhere near as big as the original, thankfully, she put her hand on the frame of the bathroom doorway to steady herself and wait it out. It was shorter and less violent but still significant.

As she stood holding the doorframe it occurred to her that if it was chaos this might be a good chance for her to escape, maybe this had knocked out the network, it might be possible to escape unnoticed. The shaking stopped and she stood still, waiting for another few moments. So far, so good. She had to find Ben.

Some hope...

Purdy gathered her essentials into her pockets once again and left her room, she figured this was one time where she could run and no one would think it odd. She got out into the square quickly and searched the faces of the people in blue all around her. It was bedlam out here. She'd never seen this many people all outside at once, it appeared as if everyone in every building had streamed out into the square since it happened.

She tried to think of a logical way to find Ben, where he might be, she instinctively made her way towards the fountain. Searching faces as she went. People were clearly frightened and upset but nowhere near what she expected. It must be the drugs again, thought Purdy, well maybe this was a somewhat good thing, at least people weren't having complete hysterics. No one seemed to be hurt which is pretty miraculous, she hoped there weren't wounded people inside the buildings. She made a deal with herself if she couldn't find Ben she would at least go back to the Blue Mansion and check to make sure there were no people who needed help, it seemed the least she could do considering she wasn't drugged up after all.

Face after face, no sign of Ben, she was beginning to feel disheartened, and just as she was about to give up he appeared in front of her. She was about to speak to him, he made a small head shaking movement, barely perceptible and Purdy was reminded of his warning to her not to acknowledge they knew each other in front of anyone else. She watched him put his hand on the shoulder of another man who was standing alone and staring at the fountain, he spoke to the man, who nodded and said thanks.

He came towards Purdy, she wasn't sure what to do, she looked away, towards the fountain. He reached her and held out his hand, holding her left arm as he had done those times before.

"Are you ok, Miss? Do you need any help?" Purdy contemplated her answer.

"I.. I'm ok I think, just a bit shaken." she unintentionally quipped. A brief smiled curled in the corner of Ben's mouth.

"Good, good." he responded then in a low voice with his lips barely moving her continued "We can't talk now, but I think we might be able to use this to our advantage, sit tight I'm trying to come up with a plan."

Purdy nodded, relieved that Ben was on the same page as her. And with that he squeezed her arm and let go, he went on to speak to another couple of people and then he was gone. She stood there a little while and then remembered her plan to go and check if people were ok. She walked back to the Blue Mansion and started walking the hallways calling out to see if anyone replied. She kept calling aloud, asking if anyone could hear her, if anyone was in need of help. She got no responses. She hoped this was good and that no one was lying crushed under bits of furniture unable to move. She turned a corner and called out again. She stopped in her tracks.

"Oh hello!" she managed; Jenny was stood blocking her way "are you ok?"

"Yes I'm fine," Jenny's eyes narrowed "What are you doing?"

"I'm checking if there's anyone who needs help, just in case, I wouldn't want anyone to be trapped or hurt, if I can help I'd like to." Purdy responded pleasantly.

"Well that's not up to you, is it?" Jenny seemed agitated.

"Not up to me?" Purdy was surprised by Jenny's unreasonable tone, she was only offering to help after all.

"Yes, they have systems in place, you're not required. Besides, we are all supposed to be going back to our rooms."

"Are we? Who said that?" Purdy felt bold, she'd had enough of Jenny and whatever happened now she was sure bowing down to Jenny's whim was not going to help her in any way.

"They... er" Jenny spluttered, she seemed unable to find the words and then luckily for her she was interrupted by an announcement that seemed to come from nowhere. Purdy looked around her, there was nothing to indicate any loud speakers but it sounded like that was where the voice was coming from.

"All residents are respectfully asked to return to their rooms until further notice. All residents are respectfully asked to return to their rooms until further notice." The message was repeated again five times.

"See," Jenny looked smug "Go on then, back to your room, I'm going to mine."

I bet you're not, thought Purdy.

"OK, OK, I'm going, jeez" Purdy waltzed off to her room, filing past all the other inhabitants of the Blue Mansion who were coming in from the square, following the instructions like good little drugged up zombies.

She got into her room and shut the door. Sitting on the bed she wondered why they'd all been ordered back inside. Maybe this was a good sign that something had broken down and she and Ben might have a chance to use that to their advantage.

She sat there for a little while and then she heard a noise outside. Quiet at first and then it got louder, it sounded familiar but out of place. She went to the window to have a look, yes! She was right, it was the sound of two helicopters coming in low over The Facility. People from the outside! Oh happy day, maybe this would be the savior for all of them, maybe the whole place was about to be busted. Purdy felt giddy with hopeful expectation. She watched the helicopters flying over the square, hiding herself behind the blue curtains so as not to be seen by anyone on the outside.

One of the helicopters looked like an ambulance, the type that the search and rescue team use, the other was smaller, Purdy squinted to see if she could make out the inhabitants. Maybe it was a rescue team? This was the initial wave and more would come? She was filled with hopeful excitement. Maybe this was going to be fine after all. It was dusk, the sun was disappearing from the sky, she could hope that darkness would provide extra cover for another escape attempt.

A little while later there was another knock at her door. Bloody Jenny, she thought, what was it now? She went over and opened the door in an angry tug, on the defense in case Jenny started on her. To her pleasant surprise, Ben was standing there, he quickly pushed past her and ran into her bathroom. She closed the door and followed him into the small room. He turned on the shower and grabbed her chipped arm.

"Hey, how you doing?" he asked.

"I'm good, good, did you see the helicopters? Do you think they've come to save us all?" they were speaking in hushed tones but Purdy was struggling to contain her excitement.

"Ah, Purdy, I don't think so to be honest. I think that ambulance has likely come to pick up an organ or a donor maybe, the earthquake may have interrupted a delicate operation. I'm not sure what the other helicopter is, it could be an escort that's providing extra support. But no, I don't think they've come to help us at all. Sadly." He could see the disappointment in her face.

"Oh," her excitement drained from her as well. "Any other ideas yet? Do you think we can try to escape tonight under the chaos of it all?"

Purdy became aware that the bathroom was fast getting dark. She reached over to flip the light on, nothing happened. She flicked the switch again, nothing.

"I think the earthquake has knocked the power out." she said.

Ben tried the switch, Purdy found this funny, like he thought she didn't know how to switch her own bathroom light on.

"Check the light in the other room." he urged her. She walked into the room and tried the light switch in there, nothing happened, she went back to the bathroom and shrugged at Ben, shaking her head.

"A power cut could be really helpful, we'll have to move quickly though, who knows how long it will be out for." she nodded her agreement. "The problem is, we're just really conspicuous in these clothes, if we only had some regular street clothes we might be able to get away and stand a chance. In these things we're like big beacons to them."

It dawned on Purdy that this was likely at least part of the reason they were all dressed in the same outfit here, it would be easy to spot a runaway. She'd not seen her own clothes since that night she was taken. And only yellow, blue, black and red outfits since.

"What if we got hold of part of a black outfit and mixed it up, would that work?" she had a sudden brain wave.

"Hmm, it might. But I don't know how we'd do that. Everyone is confined to their own buildings, I doubt we could get into the white building and convince someone to give up some of their clothes to us, and it's not like we have the time to take a pregnant woman with us, even if we could get her to understand all this. Good thought though."

Purdy thought about the people she knew, they were all in blue uniforms though, except for Chuck but she didn't know where poor Chuck would be now. It's a shame, Derek and Ben were likely the same size, that might have worked. Wait, Derek!

"I've got it!" Purdy was excited again. "Remember the plays? The theater has a wardrobe of regular street clothes, what if we snuck in there? They won't be performing anything tonight with no electricity, and there's not likely to be anyone in there to notice us right now."

"Oh that might just work!" Ben was excited too now. "Purdy Sinclair you may just be a genius!" She beamed at him.

Plan B

Purdy turned off the shower and applied her patch over her chip again. Ben stayed in the bathroom and she gingerly opened the door to see if anyone was in the hallway. The coast looked clear and there was only emergency lighting along the edges of the floor, there must be a generator for emergencies, which would make sense as both the white house and the red house would likely need emergency power for medical purposes. The Blue Mansion only received the basics from the generator, lights to make sure inmates didn't trip over in the hallway.

Purdy beckoned Ben and he swiftly darted past her into the hallway. They quickly made their way outside, sticking to the dark shadows and with no light in the square they deftly made their way across to the Art Building, no other soul was to be seen in the square and no sign of any drones. As luck would have it, the power had seemingly gone off whilst the automatic door to the Art building was set to open, the doors were wide open to them. Similarly to the Blue Mansion, the Art building had low emergency lighting that lit the way to the theater. They ran inside towards the auditorium.

They both were on the look out for drones, carefully listening out for the telltale buzz. The Robo-waiter style robots were docked along the wall but showed little evidence of being powered up. They were still eery, though, like evil statues that could come to life at any moment and strike. They were wary of disturbing them so passed by carefully and as quietly as they possibly could. Once they reached the door of the auditorium, they realized that they seemed to have made it that far unnoticed, and both of them began to relax a little. Ben was enjoying the thrill, Purdy was enjoying the thought of freedom.

Once in the theater they were in relative darkness. There was only emergency lighting in the auditorium, the stage was absolutely black. They stood in silence listening to make sure they were alone, it was absolutely silent in there, if anyone else was in there they weren't even breathing. After a minute or so, Purdy pulled out her phone and turned on the flashlight and they used it to make their way up the steps of the stage and through the curtain. Once behind it, Purdy shone her flashlight around.

"Where do you think they keep the wardrobe?" Ben whispered

"Dressing rooms, maybe? I think Derek said they were upstairs, do you see any steps?"

She shone her flashlight around the dark stage. There was an opening which looked like it led to the back stage area, she walked towards it shining the light at the floor to make sure they didn't trip, Ben followed so closely behind she could feel his breath on her neck. From the opening they could see a set of steps leading down to an area with scenery propped up in in and on the other side was a staircase.

"There!" Ben grabbed the hand she was holding the phone with and shone it directly at the stairs he'd noticed. They quickly made their way to the staircase. The good thing about it being a theater was they could move fairly silently through it, it was made in a way to limit what the audience could hear coming from backstage, the downside being it was also made to be completely dark like a blackout back there, finding their way around without lights when neither of them had been there before was tricky and potentially death defying.

Halfway up the steps, Purdy tripped and lost her balance, her hand closest to the handrail was the one holding her phone, in a moment of panic she chose not to drop the phone as it was their only source of light and her hand was frozen by fear, gripping it tightly. If it wasn't for Ben's proximity to her and his fast reactions when he heard her trip, she would have slipped through the wide spaced banister. With one smooth move he wrapped his arm around her waist and stopped her from plunging onto the concert floor below them. As she struggled to regain her composure she tried to control her racing heart and block out the thought of what might have happened whilst Ben still clung to her. After a brief moment of manic what if scenarios running through her head she shook it off, no point dwelling, she indicated to Ben she was ok and he loosened his grip on her allowing them to continue on up the stairs.

At the top of the stair case were three partially open doors, Purdy shone the light into the first one. There were men's clothes thrown everywhere, bingo! This must but Derek's dressing room, she recalled him complaining at how messy his fellow roommates were. They went inside and started rifling through the clothes. Ben found a pair of jeans he thought would likely fit and a shirt which fitted snugly. He changed into them quickly. Purdy contemplated trying to find some womenswear but as time was of the essence she just decided to pick something from in here. She also found a pair of jeans, they were made for a man so sat low on her hips but at one point that had been a trend called boyfriend jeans in the real world so she could work with that look. She also found a sweater and pulled that on. It wasn't the most glamorous look but who cared, this was about escaping, not a fashion parade.

"No turning back now…" Ben warned "We'll be leaving our blue uniforms behind, if we get caught there'll be no way of sneaking back again this time. You still in? We doing this?"

"Hell yes!" without even needing to think about it Purdy was in, this could be their last chance she was 100% in, no question about it.

They made their way back through the dark theater, carefully navigating the stairs, this time Purdy ensuring she held onto the handrail to avoid any more slips, slinking back across the stage, they waited briefly and listened before making their way out into into the auditorium again to make sure no one had joined them. They stopped and listened at the door before opening it too. No drones or other questionable noises, they snuck out into the main Art building again. The robo-waiters were all still unmoving, they moved slickly past them and out into the square again. They'd already agreed to try the same route from the night before, between the red and blue buildings, to run along the line of trees and attempt to get out of the fence before the power was fully restored.

They started to make their way across the square, sticking to the shadows. Suddenly they heard voices, Ben pulled Purdy between the Art building and the red building and they stood perfectly still trying to make out where the voices were coming from. As their eyes adjusted to the darkness without the flashlight again they made out some figures standing and talking in low voices right outside the red building. There was no way they could get past them without being spotted.

Ben tugged Purdy's sleeve to get her to follow him between the Art and red buildings. They followed the road sticking to the dark edges. This road, like the other one was also carved out between trees so they stuck to that side. Listening out for drones and more voices, so far so good.

As they walked further along the road another noise caught their attention and they stopped fast, pushing themselves into a tree to avoid being seen. This time it was the sound of an engine starting and then the familiar whirl of rotor blades, they must be starting up the helicopters again, getting them ready to leave. Purdy and Ben walked quietly between the trees, they moved quickly, and the noise got louder and louder, they must be close to it now.

They came to a clearing where the smaller of the two helicopters was sat, unattended, with the rotors in full swing. Staying in the shadow of the trees, Ben checked out the area as Purdy stood watch. There was no sign of any person out here, they must have started the engine and gone to get something. Feeling emboldened by the apparent abandonment of the flying machine, Ben trotted over and took a look in the cockpit, no sign of any people in it either. He did, however, find a handgun on the seat, he grabbed it and placed it in the waistband of the back of his jeans. He ran back to Purdy, deciding not to mention the gun to her whilst he sprinted back.

"No sign of anyone around," he spoke loudly enough to be heard over the engines without shouting.

Purdy let out a small sigh of relief. She looked at the spinning rotors of the helicopter.

"If only I knew how to fly one of those," Ben continued "sweet ride just hanging out waiting for us to take advantage, how hard do you think it is? Maybe I could give it a shot..."

"Yeh it's not easy, I don't think you could just pick it up, it took me three hours to master my hover." Purdy responded, still looking at the rotors.

Ben turned to look at her with curiosity "Wait... could you fly it?"

Purdy lacked confidence but did she really lack ability? Could she remember, she quickly went through the steps in her head, surely she could remember more than she had forgotten. If only she'd taken that helicopter flight training in the Augmented Reality Studio, if only she hadn't been kidnapped. This thought gave her a surge of confidence, those bastards had brought her here for no reason, she would make damn sure they paid and if she had to steal a helicopter to do it then that's what she had to do.

"Well, I haven't done it for a few years but I think I can remember the basics..." Purdy's voice faltered, she wasn't that confident about it but she quite liked how impressed Ben was currently looking and she was feeling determined. "What do you think? Worth a try?"

"Well I'm game if you are." he grinned at her. "And at least in the air we'll be safe from further after shocks!"

Purdy contemplated that last statement, she guessed that was true but landing might be tricky if there was widespread devastation to places flat enough to land on. She quickly put the negative thoughts to the back of her head, they needed to escape after all. It was settled, they were flying out of there... or they would crash and burn, one way or the other they would be finishing this tonight.

Like riding a bike

Taking a thorough look around, checking one last time for anyone who might see them and with no sign of any other person nearby they both sprinted towards the helicopter. Jumping inside, Purdy looked around and found two spare headsets hanging on hooks towards the back. She gave one set to Ben and showed him where to plug it in, doing the same for herself with the other set. She looked at the panel ahead of her and around the cockpit in general to familiarize herself with the layout. Things were just as she remembered, she put her left hand on the collective and her right hand grabbed the cyclic between her legs, her feet balanced on the peddles.

It was dark so she was going to have to rely on the instruments on the panel ahead of her, she reacquainted herself with the dials, hoping she recalled what they all did, she noticed the attitude indicator which would show her an artificial horizon if she couldn't see one in the dark and was happy to see a gauge which would show which direction she was flying, she presumed San Francisco would be west from here but hopefully lit up landmarks would help her with that. Maybe she could rely on Ben to help her whilst she concentrated on actually keeping them in the air.

Ben was still looking out of the windows, to check for anyone coming, he felt a little safer in the knowledge that he had the gun but didn't want to use it if he didn't have to. He pulled it out of his waist band, it had some weight to it so he assumed when he picked it up it had been loaded but he thought it wise to check for sure. He pulled out the magazine, and looking at the indicator on the back of it he saw it was fully loaded with ten bullets. He then slid the top open, seeing there was one in the chamber too he put the safety on and just held onto it whilst he continued his watch. Purdy noticed it out of the corner of her eye.

"What the…?" she said into the microphone on her headset "Where the hell did you get that from?"

"It was on the seat." he replied "Don't worry about it, I wasn't planning to use it unless we really have to, now come on let's go go go!"

"Alright, alright, I'm just getting my bearings!" she wasn't happy about the gun but now was not the time to kick up a fuss.

"Can I help, is this the handbrake, should we take it off?" Purdy knew without even looking he was talking about the collective.

"NO!" she scolded "Don't touch anything, I've got this. That's the power, not the brake!"

Ben felt suitably chastised and chose not to reply, continuing surveying the clearing around them. Purdy opened the throttle completely, she knew that when this increased the speed of the rotor it was going to sound louder and this would tip off anyone on the ground that someone was about to take off, so in turn she knew she had to move super swiftly if they were going to get away and that was going to take concentration.

She slowly pulled up the collective whilst depressing her left pedal to counteract the torque of the main rotor, her mind was reeling and her old instructor's voice echoed in her head, reminding her of the things she needed to do. If she made it out of here alive she was going to call that instructor and thank her for saving her life. Soon enough the helicopter was leaving the ground very slowly, the cyclic in her right hand became more sensitive and she pushed it forward; the back of the helicopter jerked upwards, she pulled back a little and the front came up too, it was more sensitive that she remembered and she concentrated on trying to make the ride as smooth as possible.

Ben held on for dear life, maybe he'd been wrong to place his faith in Purdy after all, these jerky movements were not filling him with a lot of confidence. By this time they were about five feet off the ground and he suddenly spotted a guy running towards them. He was reaching into his jacket, presumably going for his gun, he seemed surprised not to find it there, Ben was relieved it must be this guy's gun he found on the seat. The guy stopped running when he saw he couldn't catch them but he started shouting. Presumably he had others with him.

"Any chance we can go faster?" Ben urged.

Purdy ignored him, she was going as fast as she could. She was concentrating so much on flying that she didn't see the guy on the ground, which was probably for the best, that only would have added to her nervousness. Ben kept watch, three more figures came running out of the trees, he got the gun ready as he suspected these guys likely had guns of their own. Seeing him point the gun towards the ground spurred Purdy on. Bloody hell, how did she end up trying to fly a helicopter away from a gun fight? Never in a million years had this ever been a consideration in her quiet, pen pushing world.

"Who are they?" Purdy was flustered.

"Well, this gun's a Glock, based on that and how they look I'd suspect they were a private security guard... and we just took their helicopter, we need to get out of here, like now!"

Ten seconds later they were above tree height and Purdy started to increase the speed, pushing the helicopter forward. She checked her instruments, she moved the cyclic slightly to turn to due west. If anyone was firing guns at them so far they'd not been hit as far as she could tell and soon enough they'd be out of reach.

"I'm going to go west, is that right?" Purdy asked hoping Ben would have an answer, he was still staring down at the ground with the gun cocked towards it, so far he hadn't fired a shot.

"Uh, yeh. I mean, well its southwest actually but..." Purdy moved again to point them towards southwest, she was picking up speed now and the feel of piloting was coming back to her again, Ben pulled back from the window, satisfied that they were out of the line of fire now and he put the safety back on his gun, and put it down in his lap, marveling at how quickly they had risen above tree level. "Wow, you're doing an amazing job, you've really not done this for years?"

"Nope!" Purdy grinned to herself. "Thanks. How far are we from San Francisco?"

"Only about 30 miles, as the crow flies." Ben was looking out of the window for any landmarks he could direct her towards. "Look there! See? Do you see the Golden Gate Bridge?"

Purdy looked where Ben was pointing, sure enough, there on the horizon she saw the distinctive suspension bridge lit up, she was thankful that tonight was not a foggy one, otherwise it might have been impossible to spot.

"Yup, got it, I'm heading that way!" Purdy was getting excited again, maybe freedom would be hers again after all! "Oh Ben, this is amazing, thank you so much for helping me! I can't wait to get home. Do you live near here? After all this is over you should come over and we'll celebrate!"

"Purdy, we still have to get you to the Consulate, you remember?" Ben replied after a brief pause.

"Yeh, yeh I know, 1 Sansome street. Get to the Consulate, I mean after this is all sorted and I get back to my little house at Buena Vista Park, ooh if we go close enough maybe I can point it out you..."

"Focus! Our only goal is getting to safety right now, not sightseeing." Ben was firm.

"I know... I was kidding..." Purdy's attempt to lighten the mood with humor apparently fell flat.

"We've got to get you to the Consulate so they can protect you. You won't be able to stay here, Purdy, you're going to have to return to the UK, it's the only way you'll be safe, otherwise they'll just come after you again." he said gently.

Purdy took this in. It hadn't occurred to her that this was it, this was going to force her to go home-home. She hadn't prepared herself for that and wasn't sure of her feelings about it. For now she was going to file it away in the back of her mind, worry about that after she was safe and in the Consulate.

"Ok" she said, feeling deflated, then turned her mind to practical matters "So, any ideas where we're going to land this?"

"I have a feeling we can land a Pier 29, I vaguely remember seeing it on a helipad map of San Francisco once when I worked for the SFPD." Ben responded.

"Oh. So you're a cop?" Purdy was intrigued.

"I was. A long time ago." was his response, it was quite obvious he was in no mood to talk about it further so she didn't pry any more.

They sat in silence, Purdy concentrating on flying the helicopter, Ben looking out for landmarks he could point her towards.

"Ben…" Purdy began after a short while.

"Yeh?" He continued watching out of the window.

"Who's doing all this? Who owns The Facility?"

Ben sighed. "It's owned by a conglomerate of wealthy people, people so wealthy that they can buy anything they like."

"Is the government involved?" she asked, considering firstly her own position, presuming the government must know if she was going to have to leave the country, and secondly what she could do, if she survives, to help everyone else.

"They're not involved, as such." Ben responded "They're just complicit with it. Turn a blind eye, you might say. They reap the benefit as it seems like their administration is hitting it out of the park, record employment, record lows in crime rates and The Facility, and other facilities just like it all over the country, deal with things that mean they don't have to. It saves them tax dollars so they can make the tax payers happy and there's really no one around to complain. Except our resistance group and we have to work very covertly to avoid being found out."

Purdy gulped, she'd been living that blissfully ignorant high life, low tax, low crime, happy existence. If she had known it had come at such a cost, the cost of the lives of others, more unfortunate than her, would she still have had such a happy existence? She couldn't go back to life as she'd known it before The Facility that was for sure.

"Maybe, if I make it safely back to England, maybe I will be able to spread the word? To help your resistance?" she said hopefully.

"Maybe..."

"Ben?" she began again

"Mmhmm?"

"You've seen my file, right? Do you know the name of the person that I was supposed to be a donor for?" Ben was quiet and didn't answer immediately. "Ben? Do you?"

"I do. But I don't think it is productive for us to talk about it now. Let's talk about it later, eh?" he really sounded like it wasn't something he could get into right now which just made her suspicious.

"Is it someone I know? Someone well known?" he didn't answer and she realized he wasn't going to give the information up no matter how much she asked. "Ok, I get it, maybe we can talk about it after we land.

"Maybe…" Ben didn't sound enthusiastic but she convinced herself he was just distracted by their predicament, suddenly his voice changed and she heard an edge of excitement to it. "Let's just concentrate on getting you to that Consulate for now, shall we?! Look! We're getting closer, see!"

Purdy had settled into flying mode and was pleased it was going better than she could have imagined so she took a moment to check out the landmarks Ben was excited about. The Golden Gate Bridge was getting larger and more distinct as they headed that direction, she could also see the Bay Bridge and the San Francisco skyline. The Ferry Building was lit up, she wasn't sure which direction pier 29 was and was about to ask when a red light lit up on the panel in front of her.

"Uh oh. We've only got a gallon of fuel left. I suspect that's where the pilot had disappeared off to, they needed to refuel the helicopter for their journey." Purdy was trying to stay calm, she wasn't even sure how far that one gallon of fuel would take them.

"I think we need a back up plan in case we don't make it to Pier 29" Ben was trying to stay calm too "erm, what happens if we run out of gas while we're flying? Does the engine stop?"

"It's ok if we run out of fuel mid air," Purdy assured him "we can always do can autorotation landing..." she hoped not though, she was terrified at the prospect of landing in good conditions, without an engine was just going to add another layer of complexity to the situation.

"Think we can make it to Treasure Island?" Ben pointed down to the island which sat out in the Bay, jutting away from Yerba Buena Island which was highlighted by the prominence of the Bay Bridge spanning out of each side of it.

"I think we've maybe got another five minutes of flying in us on this tank, so that's the extreme of what we could make." Purdy sounded more confident than she felt.

"OK, make for Treasure Island then, we can only hope for the best."

Purdy pointed them towards the island and decided she was going to try and cruise them down slowly, like an airplane, and land in the first open space she found. Trying to be too clever and bring them down in a confined space was likely to end in disaster. If all else failed she considered ditching them in the Bay, although it would be freezing and after all this, dying of hyperthermia was not the optimum result. On the upside, all that swimming she had been doing might actually pay off if she needed to make a swim for it.

They were getting lower and coming in close to the island, ahead of them was a large open field like area with what looked like a football pitch marked out on it, perfect! Purdy was relieved, this was where she would aim for. She'd slowed their progress and was beginning to feel relaxed when the fuel ran out. Not to worry, this would be fine.

"Uh, Purdy, you got this? Should I brace or something?"

"Yep, got this, you should brace anyway, it's going to be bumpy." Purdy could see the ground coming and it wasn't so fast that she was nervous, she was just going to pull back on the cyclic to level them off. She realized Ben had closed his eyes and, knowing the landing might be bumpy but pretty sure they were going to be fine she decided to have some fun with him. "You can swim, right?"

"What?!" Ben opened is eyes in fright just to see as Purdy brought the helicopter down with a bump. Not the smoothest landing but they were on the ground. Purdy's whole body felt heavy with the pent up tension and her hands stayed firmly around the controls. Her muscles relaxed but her entire being throbbed with adrenaline. She couldn't believe they'd survived this far.

5 miles to go

They sat in stunned silence whilst the blades were slowing down. Ben took off his headset and pulled Purdy's off the back of her head where it had slid when she leaned forward after the landing.

"You are amazing!" Ben was overjoyed. "You OK?"

Purdy was slumped forward in her seat with her head resting gently on the cyclic. She genuinely couldn't believe she had managed that, but apparently once you learn it, you never forget it. She lifted her head and nodded at grinning Ben, she needed a moment to collect herself.

"OK, no time to sit on our laurels! First things first, let's get rid of that awful chip from your arm." he pulled out a Swiss Army knife from his shoe. Of course Ben had a Swiss Army knife, he was the sort of man who would never be without one, she wondered how in the hell he had kept it hidden but didn't have the energy to ask.

He pulled out a sharp blade and tugged the neck of her sweater down over her left shoulder. Purdy was complicit, she wanted rid of the chip and the fact that her gruesome nude bra was on display didn't phase her at all. Ben pulled off the copper patch gently.

"This is going to hurt but I'm going to be as gentle as I can" and with that he stuck the point of the knife into her skin and flipped out the tiny chip into his hand. Purdy winced at the pain but didn't make a fuss, she was just glad that violation was out of her body. "We'll leave this in the helicopter. If they are tracking you down it will lead them here. In fact, have you still got your phone on you?" Purdy pulled it out of her pocket and Ben switched it all the way off. "They can't track that either now, right we have to get away and into the City right now."

Ben opened the door to step out, the rotors had slowed significantly now and posed little risk as long as he kept aware of them. Purdy pulled her sweater up onto her shoulder again and pulled herself together. They were so close now, she just had to keep it together until they got downtown. She was disappointed they weren't closer to their destination but was hoping Ben had a plan to get them there.

She stepped out of her side of the helicopter, taking care to avoid the blades and they both jogged towards the edge of the football pitch.

"So, you've got a plan right?" Purdy said breathlessly to Ben, "I mean I feel I did my bit getting us this far." she was joking but also feeling bloody proud of herself and her abilities, Ben beamed at her.

"You absolutely did, without you we probably wouldn't have got out of there. I don't actually have a fully formed plan yet, but I'm thinking we need to find a car."

"We could call an Uber..." Purdy thought aloud.

"Yeh, we could but right now I don't know that we can trust that an Uber would get you where you need to go, we can't turn your phone on as it is likely being tracked and any Uber would probably just take you right back to The Facility anyway. I'm taking you myself. I'm going to find a car."

Purdy was flattered he'd taken it upon himself to be her knight in shining armor but finding and taking a car was easier said than done. There were plenty of cars about but she'd heard they were impossible to steal now that they were self driving and could be summoned by an app on the owner's phone. Not that Purdy had ever been in the habit of stealing cars before they were self driving but this was one of the features that enabled self driving cars to become accepted and adopted so widely. Of course, then crime rates went down anyway for reasons

Purdy had recently discovered so maybe it wasn't that hard to steal a car, its just that nobody tried anymore. She considered asking Ben just as he grabbed her hand and started pulling her away.

"Quick, this way, I hear a car engine, we might be lucky."

They ran across the street and down a road named Gateview Avenue. A street just off of that avenue had a row of cars parked along the side of it. Music was coming from a nearby house and they could hear what sounded like laughter and a party going on. Just outside the house was a woman, talking furiously into her phone, it sounded like she was having a lovers tiff and whoever was on the other end was in a lot of trouble for something.

The woman was walking up and down the driveway, screaming and crying into her phone. Nearby was the car with the engine started, Ben pointed it out to Purdy. They ran quietly along the dark street so as to remain undetected by the shrieking woman. They got to the car and looked in the window, no one was inside. Purdy tried the back door and it was unlocked, Ben whispered to her to get inside. She snuck in and laid across the back seat, waiting for Ben to get in the front. She wondered if working for Triple A he had picked up tips on how to steal a car without the owner's phone.

It seemed to be taking ages for Ben to join her in the car. The woman appeared to have finally stopped shrieking, maybe he was trying to stay unnoticed now she wasn't so distracted. Purdy was about to take a sneaky look out of the window when she heard the front door open. She was relieved and was just about to ask him where he'd been when she got a sudden whiff of perfume, she froze. It wasn't Ben getting in, it was the angry, shrieking woman. Of course it made sense that this was her car.

The woman docked her phone and told the console to drive home. Purdy lay there motionless, she considered her options. She could sit up now and tell the woman she made a mistake, get out and look for Ben, then again what if the woman locked the doors and she couldn't get out? She could call the police. This was maybe a bad plan. She had no idea where 'home' was for this woman, but if it was in San Francisco she would be one step closer to freedom. From where she lay it was going to be impossible to see, for now she would bide her time. She was worried about Ben but she knew he would tell her that her that she just needed to get to the Consulate, he could take care of himself and Purdy felt she had to take care of herself now too.

"Call Nick!" Purdy jumped as the woman shouted at her phone, maybe Nick was who she was just having the shouting match with, oh well if the woman was shrieking at the phone at least she would be less likely to notice her stowaway in the back seat.

After a couple of of rings the video console on the dash lit up and another woman's face appeared.

"Hey Caz, what's up?"

"Nick, I'm so frigging angry!" Caz began "Dave was supposed to meet me at Twinkie's birthday party at her place on Treasure Island but he stood me up! I've had about as much as I can take from him, I'm so over it, who does he think he is? I'm way out of his league anyway..."

Caz continued on her self pitying rant whilst Nick it seemed just listened. Purdy got the impression that this was likely not the first one of these rants that Nick had endured based on her silence and apparent unwillingness to interject with her own thoughts.

"... and after that huge frigging earthquake today, Twinkie's lucky I ventured out to that landfill hell-hole, I mean I was putting my own life at risk going out there, which was one of Dave's excuses, he claims he's had to go over to see his Mom as she's had a power cut and needs his help..." Caz was still ranting on, Purdy thought Dave sounded like a good man for choosing to go help his mother rather than go to a party with this angry woman, maybe her dumping him was going to be quite a relief for him.

Purdy stretched her neck up to see if she could see any sign of where they were going, taking care not to put herself into Caz's peripheral vision or in front of the dash camera to avoid Nick noticing her too. It was dark and from this angle she couldn't see anything useful.

"… and I turned Tony down, he asked me to meet him in the Castro tonight, but nooo, out of loyalty to Dave I declined, that was foolish, I should just go and meet Tony!" It sounded like Caz was forming a new plan for her evening.

"Yeh…" Nick finally got a word in "I totally agree, show Dave what he's missing! Go meet Tony and then snapchat the whole night, that'll show him!" oh this Nick sounded just as bad as Caz, but if she convinced Caz to go to the Castro at least Purdy would definitely know she was going to San Francisco, as long as she wasn't talking about Castro Valley, that would not help her plight.

"Uh, I don't know. I mean, I'm mad with Dave but I don't want it to end, he does have a Ferrari and a house in Pacific Heights after all…" Purdy rolled her eyes to herself at the shallowness of this woman, Dave did sound like a catch though, loves his mum and has his own money... although, she wondered, maybe the money was his mothers and he just was keeping her sweet to keep his lifestyle, such supposition, she mused to herself, she had no idea anything about these peoples' lives really!

"Well you could go out with Tony and not snapchat it..." presumably Nick's point was if Dave didn't see it on social media then Caz could get away with having some fun behind his back with Tony, this girl sounded delightful, Purdy thought sarcastically.

"Hmm... well I am looking hot tonight, it seems a shame to waste it on going straight home..."

"Yeh, you do look really hot!" Purdy was gagging at the pair of them, had young women always been this shallow? Or was this down to the curse of their entire lives having played out on social media since their parents first posted their sonogram pictures on Facebook, through their childhoods being publicized on Instagram, to their teenage and young adult lives being lived completely through selfies. What a sad, superficial world this had become, maybe Purdy had been better off in The Facility... no, no she hadn't, the world had not lost hope and she should not lose focus.

"I'm doing it! OK, talk to you later!" Caz hung up the phone "Castro and Market, please!" she barked at the console. The car didn't change direction so Purdy assumed they were heading towards San Francisco anyway, she breathed out a sigh of relief as silently as she could.

So near and yet so far

Caz put on some music and turned the volume up, Purdy peeked over the front seat to see her pull out a compact and start fixing her make up whilst she jigged along in her seat in time to the music. She seemed distracted enough for Purdy to take a chance and glance out of the window. From the small view she got it seemed they were still on the Bay Bridge.

Castro and Market wasn't a bad place for her to end up. It was likely about a three mile walk from there to 1 Sansome which she could handle. Although it occurred to her, would she be able to get into the Consulate in the middle of the night? What would she do in the meantime? Fred! Maybe she could throw herself on his mercy? He lived in that area, he'd help her, surely.

The car was slowing down, Purdy glanced up through the window and saw they were approaching the toll booth, they wouldn't stop there but the car had to slow to pass through the E-ZPass lane so the toll could be taken from Caz's account. Once they'd passed through they sped up again and continued their journey down into San Francisco. Purdy felt a flutter of excitement that she was almost at her familiar stomping ground, and considered what she might say to Fred, she desperately hoped he would be home, although she had completely lost track of what day of the week it was, she hoped he wasn't out tonight.

As the car pulled off of 101 Purdy felt the car slow and go down hill towards the light where Mission meets Duboce, she recognized it immediately from the Freeway ramp which arched off to the side of them. Her heart was racing, soon she would have to decide how to escape from the back of the car unnoticed. How hard can that be, after all? She'd flown a helicopter out of a camp guarded by technology and lunatics tonight already, a car owned by an angry, selfie taking harpy should be easy enough.

Caz was searching through her music library and settled on a song. She turned the volume up to a deafening level, Purdy recognized the tune immediately, Caz was obviously a fan of a good oldie, David Guetta's Titanium blasted out of the speakers. Purdy smiled to herself, this song brought back happy memories of a time of innocence and youth to her, she moved her leg in time to the beat waiting for Sia's vocals to kick in... only for it to be ruined by Caz adding her own voice to the mix. Dear god, that woman had a pair of lungs on her, if she wasn't using them for shouting she was belting out tunes from the early 21st century… poorly as it turned out.

The car pulled up to the light at Market street and stopped, Caz was singing her head off to the world about being bulletproof, Purdy took this as her chance to exit the car. She swiftly opened the back door and jumped out, closing it gently behind her. He ruse worked, Caz made no move that showed she'd noticed, Purdy could still hear her screeching along, the light turned green and the car pulled away, leaving Purdy standing alone on the corner of Market and Duboce. Alone for the first time since leaving The Facility, suddenly she missed Ben. Would she ever see him again? Was he ok?

Aware that it was possible that she had the face of a wanted person she put her head down and quickly made her way to Fred's house, which was nearby. Along the way she contemplated her evening. She was trying to ignore that fact that she likely would never see Ben again after losing him on Treasure Island, but she couldn't fight it in the end, the thought overwhelmed her, it was gut wrenchingly sad, tears formed in her eyes. She'd not known him long but the things they'd experienced together made her feel closer to him than any other person she'd ever met. But she didn't even know his surname. She had to accept that he was a part of her journey out of that place and nothing more. It was a miserable thought but likely true nonetheless. She didn't even care now that she'd never know who she was to be a donor for, she was just left bereft at the loss of her friend, her confidant, the one person who knew what she had been through.

She trudged along the street in the dark. Traffic on the streets was sporadic this evening, not a lot of cars around but when one passed her by she turned her head slightly away in order the hide her face. She got to the corner of Fred's street and stood waiting for the light to change in order for her to cross. In normal circumstances she wouldn't think twice about a little jay-walking but tonight she wasn't about to risk drawing negative attention to herself unnecessarily.

She heard the short burst of a police siren behind her, she jumped and tried to stay inconspicuous, after all they often made this noise when they came up to a junction that they planned to blast through. The car slowed down and came to a stop just next to her. Panic raised inside her but she stood routed to the spot. She feared she looked suspicious in not turning around so she briefly looked up at the car. The window was wound down and a police officer looked out at her. She nodded and turned away.

"Excuse me, ma'am?" oh crap, Purdy thought, she contemplated making a dash for it, "we had a report of someone skulking around this neighborhood, a man wearing all black, have you seen anyone?"

"No," Purdy shook her head.

"OK. Are you ok? Do you need help?" the police officer sounded genuinely concerned, Purdy suspected she must look out of place.

"I'm good, thanks. I'm just going to my friend's house." she tried to sound as American as she could, not wanting to draw any attention to herself with her English accent, she limited the amount she spoke.

"Is it far?"

"No, just across there in fact!" Purdy pointed vaguely further up the street than Fred's house, she really didn't want to show the police his exact house.

The light changed to walk and Purdy hesitated, she didn't want to walk off on the cop but she also didn't want to hang around.

"OK, good, well you take care of yourself!" the cop smiled and pulled away, Purdy walked quickly to the other side of the street and turned towards Fred's house. Relieved they hadn't been looking for her she felt a little more confident as she rang Fred's bell.

There was no answer, Purdy felt despondent. Maybe Fred had gone out for the evening after all. She took out her phone then remembered Ben's warning about it being tracked, she didn't dare turn it on for fear of alerting people to where she was, she put it back in her pocket. She tried the bell again, with little hope of an answer. There was a noise from within the house and then a light behind the door came on, she anxiously anticipated Fred opening the door. The door opened quickly and Purdy stood there staring at a tall, distinguished looking man with red hair whom she did not recognize.

Reunion

"Hello!" said the red headed man brightly, Purdy was suspicious, she didn't know this man, what if he was from The Facility? What if they knew Purdy would come to Fred's? He was the most contacted person in her contacts list after all this was probably the worst place she could have come; she was about to turn on her heels and sprint away.

"Who is it?" Fred's voice came from behind the red headed man and Purdy's heart leapt with joy.

"Fred!" she exclaimed.

"I don't know, it's a lady..." said the red head.

"Purdy!!" Fred pushed past him and pulled Purdy into a bear hug. She crumpled into an emotional mess in his arms.

"Oh Fred, I thought I'd never see you again..." she spluttered through sobs.

"OK drama queen, come inside." Fred made light of it but could tell his friend was traumatized by something, he helped her through the doorway with the red head closing the door behind them.

He ushered her into his living room. Just as Purdy remembered, it was perfectly tidy, perfectly stylish and perfectly welcoming in equal measure. She sat down on the large, comfy couch and Fred muted the TV which was chattering away in the corner of the room.

"You need a drink," Fred decided "Thomas, go get Purdy a vodka cocktail from the kitchen!" Thomas trotted off dutifully to get the beverage. "So, missy, where have you been hiding?"

Purdy gulped back her tears and looked at Fred.

"Who's that?" she asked in a hushed tone, nodding towards the kitchen, she'd never seen this guy before and wondered how long ago he appeared, maybe he was one of 'them' and was planted here to bring her back.

"That's Thomas... I told you about him." he had? When? "Well, I texted you about him, I planned to tell you in person but you then went and disappeared on me!" Of course, Purdy hadn't received any of Fred's actual texts whilst in The Facility, they'd been filtered and changed before they got to her. She didn't want to give up this information too readily until she was sure Thomas was kosher, and it sounded like he might not have been around for that long.

"Oh yes, that's right, Thomas," she said slowly "where did you meet again?"

"Oh Purdy, you never pay attention to me! I met him about six months ago. Of course, I played my cards close to my chest for the first couple of months as I didn't want to jinx it. Wait, you're not pretending you don't remember just because you're mad at me for not telling you earlier are you?" she shook her head. "Good. Well, we starting dating casually then after about three months I'd decided I couldn't let this one slip away, he was just too much of a catch. In fact, I had planned on telling you about him on that day you went off on your adventures. Remember I asked you to come VRing that night? I brought Thomas along so you could meet him but you stood me up!"

"Oh I'm sorry! I never meant to stand you up. But that's so lovely!" Purdy was happy for her friend and relieved that he'd known Thomas longer than she had been away.

"Yes it's been six months already, that's quite the record for me! He's moved in and everything and I'm not at all bored with him yet!"

"Six months?!" Purdy was aghast and did the calculation in her head "So, you've not seen me in three whole months?"

"No, and I have a bone to pick with you about that, how dare you just up and leave work to go on some sabbatical to find yourself without fully discussing it with me first? I did not authorize that! I might have wanted to come too! Mexico sounded amazing..."

"Sabbatical? Mexico?" so this is what The Facility changed her messages to Fred to say, no wonder he'd not been worried about her, they'd made it sound like she'd been off on a wonderful trip finding herself. She was somewhat comforted by their intimate 'I did not authorize' joke though and she smiled warmly at him, he wasn't really mad at her.

"Yes" Fred said indignantly, as if she was questioning his sanity. "When did you get back? I see you picked up no fashion tips while traveling, where *did* you get that hideous outfit? Boyfriend jeans are so 2013!"

Purdy giggled a little, oh how she'd missed Fred.

"Wow six months eh? Well I guess you'd better introduce me properly! I wish I didn't look such a mess."

"Oh you're fine... I mean, you've looked better but Thomas won't care, he's too lovely. I'm so smitten, Purd!" Fred looked super happy and whilst Purdy was still unsure that she could trust anyone right now she felt if Fred was smitten with this man he must be a good sort and she would have to tell them both everything.

Thomas returned with a vodka cocktail, grabbed a coaster, and placed them on the table next to where Purdy was sat.

"There you go." he said "Now, I'm Thomas and it's a pleasure to finally meet you, Fred talks about you all the time!" he held out a warm hand to Purdy and she shook it.

"Hi, it's so lovely to meet you, I'm sorry I turned up late at night and unannounced like this, you must think I am terrible."

"Not at all, darling, knowing how Fred feels about you it is clear to me that you should be welcome anytime and I am glad to have the chance to get to know you, no matter the hour!"

Purdy was relieved, not only was Thomas extremely pleasant but he also had an English accent, she felt sure that there was no way he could be working for The Facility as a foreigner himself. She was mesmerized by his blazing red hair, she knew red hair was a favorite of Fred's, they'd often joked about him finding a flame haired beau as every Fred needs a Ginger.

"And yes before you ask I *do* do everything Fred does, only backwards and in heels." Thomas joked, as he noted her checking out his tresses and acknowledged the unspoken Fred and Ginger reference. Purdy burst out laughing, oh yes she liked this man, he made the same silly jokes that she and Fred laughed at. As the giggling faded, the tears began to well up again.

"Hey, hey, what are the tears for? Come on, you can tell us all about it. It can't be that bad, we'll sort it out." Fred handed her a tissue.

Purdy took the deepest breath imaginable and began her story, from the medical, through the kidnap to the weeks she spent drugged up and held captive and finally on to how she met Ben and their escape in the helicopter. Fred and Thomas sat quietly through her story, asking questions and for clarifications but on the whole just letting her get the whole story off of her chest. It took hours for her to explain the whole thing. Thomas and Fred came in and out of the room bringing drink top ups and at one point they ordered a pizza as, as they told her, she looked like she needed feeding up.

It was the most delicious delivery pizza she had ever tasted. It took 45 minutes for them to deliver it, it wasn't as hot as it should have been and the cheese was a little too congealed but she enjoyed every morsel as she knew it wasn't laced with some awful mind bending drug which would take away her consciousness, her personality and her humanity. She realized how much she'd missed real life in that place of pretend perfection, where everything worked perfectly, except the human beings.

"Wait..." said Fred when Purdy showed them her arm where Ben had removed the chip. "Do you think I have one too? I have a flu shot every year, and I certainly never signed up for a chip to make payments, I always felt like that was a recipe for disaster, you're not telling me I've been chipped anyway?!"

Purdy shrugged and he pulled up the sleeve of his t-shirt for Thomas to have a look and prod around.

"I can't say for definite, but there's a lump here..." Thomas said

"Get it out! Get it out of me!" Fred was getting upset and Thomas attempted to calm him down "Why aren't you more upset? Maybe you have one too?"

"I doubt it," Thomas retorted "I haven't been to any doctors in the last decade and I never signed up for a payment chip either, there's no way they could have chipped me. Want me to try and remove it?"

Fred nodded furiously and Thomas went off to the kitchen to get a sharp knife, some antiseptic ointment and bandages. He gave Fred a vodka top up and Purdy let him squeeze her hand. Deftly Thomas got the knife and pulled out the chip, discarding it down the garbage disposal. He then patched up Fred and cleaned up Purdy's arm as well. She felt so safe here with them she didn't want to leave but she knew that even having just come here she may have endangered them by association. She apologized profusely for this.

"Nonsense, nonsense. I will not hear it, right Thomas?" Fred told her.

"Yes, of course. It is not your fault, and we would have been hurt if you'd felt you couldn't come here. We're big boys we can look after ourselves." Purdy was so glad Fred had met Thomas, they seemed such a perfect complement to each other.

"Thank you, you really are too kind." she said "Now, I really must get to the British Consulate. It's downtown, on Sansome Street, do you think I could walk it from here?"

"Well of course you could walk it but we won't hear of it, we'll take my car, I want to deposit you there myself, make sure you get there." Fred spoke firmly to her, there wasn't going to be any dissuading him.

"But Fred..." she began, but he put his hand up to silence her, there was no arguing this one.

"We shall take my car," Thomas interjected "It's less conspicuous and there's safety in numbers. We can hide you in the back, Purdy, and I'll drop you both right at the door, that way Freddie can escort you all the way in and make sure you are deposited safely, I'll wait with the car and keep a lookout for suspicious folks who might be tracking you."

"Oh Thomas, that's kind of you but I wouldn't want you to get in trouble..."

"I'll be fine, don't you worry about it." Thomas wasn't going to take no for an answer either so Purdy gave up trying.

"Would you like to take a shower and get changed before we go?" Fred asked it as a question but it sounded more like a suggestion to her really.

"Erm, I've got nothing else with me..." she began.

"It's ok, you can borrow something from us, how about some clean sweatpants and a long sleeve t shirt?"

"Sounds good to me, thanks!" Purdy followed Fred to the guest bathroom and he gave her a huge hug.

"I've missed you! Don't you ever disappear on me again, you hear?!"

Purdy was too sad to tell Fred she was going to have to leave the country, she relished his warm hug and held back her tears, that would have to wait until after she'd made it to the Consulate.

A quick trip across town

Dawn was breaking as they set off on the short journey downtown. They got into Thomas's car in the garage without needing to leave the building. Fred and Thomas got in the front after helping Purdy into the back seat where she laid down with a blanket over her. The roads were fairly quiet, with not a lot of traffic on them. Both men subtly looked around them as they went along to check for anyone watching or following them.

"So shall we grab some brunch after we've got you sorted at the Consulate?" Fred spoke to Purdy from the front of the car without turning around. She squirmed uncomfortably under the blanket.

"Let's wait and see how long it takes, shall we?" Thomas seemed to understand that Purdy was likely not going to be around for brunches anytime soon but neither of them were going to break it to Fred just yet.

"Uh, yeh, ok. Good idea, maybe lunch will be more likely..." Fred trailed off and continued to look out of the windows around them.

"OK, don't make it obvious but check out the car behind us in a sec, it's been following us since we turned out of our road but I can't make out how many people are inside..." Thomas was trying to sound calm but he seemed genuinely perturbed, Purdy's body stiffened under her blanket as she waited to hear more.

Fred leaned forward in his seat as if to tie his shoe lace and looked in the wing mirror of Thomas's car. From that angle he could see there were two people in the car, a man and a woman. They were obviously having a conversation with each other but were both staring intently at Thomas's car ahead of them. Fred leaned back again.

"Man and a woman," he said without turning his head at all "they may well be following us, hard to tell, why don't you pull off of Divis and onto a smaller side street, I'll watch them to see if they look like they're following us." he leaned forward again and kept his eye on the mirror.

Thomas made a sudden movement and turned right off of Divisadero onto Golden Gate Avenue at the last moment. Fred had to grab the dashboard to steady himself but kept an eye on the mirror, the car behind them also turned at the last minute and Fred saw the man move the steering wheel at the last second to make the car turn. This was a sure fire sign that Golden Gate Avenue was not in their original intended route, self-driving cars readjusted their routes as they go along based on information they retrieve from map services on road and traffic conditions but never do they make last second decisions without indicating first, that is always a manual override.

"Yep, they're following us. Shit." Fred said as he sat up.

"Don't panic, I'm sure we can lose them." Thomas replied with a mixture of authority and excitement in his voice. "Hold on."

Purdy couldn't see from beneath her blanket on the back seat but Fred was both shocked and in awe by what he witnessed. It turned out that the reason Thomas had insisted that they take his car was because it had a manual override mode. Most self-drive cars had, for safety reasons, the ability for the person in the driving seat to take over the steering, braking and ever so briefly, the accelerator but that was as much control as the human was given. Thomas's car on the other hand had a complete manual override because it had been purchased in another state which had not fully adopted autonomous driving yet. In addition to this, Fred and Purdy discovered that Thomas himself also had the driving skills of a Formula 1 racing driver. So *this* was the reason Thomas had insisted on driving after all, he knew Fred wouldn't have had the skill, or indeed the car, to evade their pursuers.

He took a series of right hand turns, each of them perfectly timed to miss any other traffic, and sped across intersections like he had a sixth sense with regards to the road. It was like a sight seeing tour of San Francisco in fast forward, at one point they even passed the Painted Ladies of Steiner Street. Fred clung on for dear life.

Thomas checked the rear view mirror, unfortunately the car behind was keeping up for the most part. He thought he'd lost them at one point but the car appeared again at the next intersection, they obviously knew what Purdy's destination was so Thomas decided to mix it up. They got to Geary and he turned the car to drive towards the ocean, away from downtown. The lights were all synchronized to change in order so if you hit it right you could drive about a mile without having to stop for a red one. The car behind was keeping up with them, and had moved into the middle lane, Thomas sped up and the car which was now behind and to the left of their car mirrored them. The final light was just turning red, Thomas looked as if he was about to go through the light but at the last second turned right down a small side street. The car behind was following so closely and at such speed it couldn't react in time and flew straight past the intersection.

Thomas slammed on the brakes of the car, then reversed into an alleyway, driving in a straight line through the two sides of the road with cars parked along it. When he got the the street at the end he pulled out blindly, a lady who was crossing the street jumped in fright at the sight of him.

"Terribly sorry!" Thomas called out of the window at her whilst she looked on in shock.

He sped away and into the Presidio.

"I think we lost them!" Fred exclaimed gleefully, he was both impressed and surprised by his partner's skills "Do I even want to know where you learned to drive like that?!"

Thomas just smiled to himself and when he briefly glanced at Fred he had a twinkle in his eye that revealed under his distinguished, refined, English gentleman exterior, Thomas obviously had some hidden past that Fred couldn't deny turned him on somewhat.

They drove through the Presidio and out into the Marina, there was still no sign of the car which had been following them, they relaxed a little.

"How you doing, Purd?" Fred checked in on the unusually quiet Purdy.

"I'm ok, feeling a little bit sick to be honest but coping. That was quite a ride!"

"Wasn't it though?! You're lucky you couldn't see what was going on, I've had one eye closed throughout, the speed was terrifying!" Fred was never one for any kind of danger in his life, he liked his feet on the ground and the safety of speed limits.

"Are we nearly there yet?" she asked, acknowledging that she sounded like a child in the back seat on a road trip with her parents.

"We're just on Lombard, be there in about eight minutes... hopefully." Thomas responded.

"Lombard? How'd we get there?"

"Don't ask," said Fred " but don't worry, I think we can avoid going down the crooked bit!" he was amused by their sight seeing trip, regardless of the terror he felt.

Thomas drove quickly through the city and as promised within eight minutes they were pulling onto Sansome street. It was still early and the streets were still quiet, deserted apart from one person leaning up against the wall outside of the Consulate.

"OK, I think we may have another obstacle." Thomas suggested as he clocked the woman leaning against the wall.

"Nah," Fred said, "She's just waiting for someone, surely?"

"What? Who's just waiting?" Purdy was frustrated that she still couldn't see anything.

"There's a woman leaning against the wall near to the door of the Consulate." Thomas informed her. "I suspect she may be looking for you, she looks out of place, and there's no one else around, it seems odd that someone would just be waiting there at this time of the morning."

"Yeh, I dunno," said Fred "She just looks like she's hanging out to me."

"No sense in taking chances, I've got a plan." Thomas was full of surprises, hot shot driver and a man with a plan, what *did* this man do for a living? "I'll go over and speak to her, ask her directions, once I've got her attention, you two make a run for the door. OK?"

"OK" Purdy came out from under the blanket but made sure to stay below the window so she couldn't be seen from the street.

"Once you're inside, they can't touch you, you'll technically be on British soil." Purdy didn't know if that was actually technically true but Thomas said it with such conviction that she was willing to believe it. "OK, darling, it has been wonderful to meet you, hopefully the next time we meet it will be under much better circumstances, you take care of yourself."

"Thank you for everything, Thomas, it's been great meeting you too, I hope you don't get in any trouble because of me..."

"Silence, lovely girl, all will be well with the world. Good luck!"

Thomas pulled the car over to the side of the street, winked at Fred and got out. He strolled over to the woman like a man with purpose. Fred and Purdy just overheard him saying "Excuse me..." quite loudly then his voice became indecipherable.

"OK" said Fred "Let's give him a couple of minutes then we'll open the doors on the left side of the car together, get out in the street and make a run for it to the door, sound like a plan?"

"Yup, sounds like a plan, you just let me know when to go." She said peeking up at him from her position on the back seat. "Hey Fred"

"Yeh?"

"Where on earth did you find Thomas? And where did he learn such skills?!"

"Ha!" Fred turned his head and with a glint in his eye he continued, "I've got no idea! It's hot, though, isn't it?"

"Very…" Purdy had to concur and Fred chuckled.

"Ok, you ready?"

"Ready as I'll ever be!"

"Alright, go!" Purdy fumbled with the back door as Fred got out the front, after the initial failure she managed to get the door open and they were both running for the door to the Consulate.

Out of nowhere a man came running straight towards Purdy, Fred grabbed her hand and pulled her along. They reached the door and he banged on it, the door began to open as the man caught up to them and grabbed Purdy's sweater, Fred pushed her in through the door and blocked the man's way. A military guard wearing fatigues and holding a large rifle on the other side of the door caught hold of Purdy.

"I'm British" she managed to gasp "I need your help!"

The man still had his hand on Purdy's sweater.

"I suggest you let the lady go." said the huge Guard who was now holding her around the waist. The man let go and pulled Fred away.

"Fred!" she shouted.

"I'll be fine, you go, go" he called back as he was dragged away from the door.

British Bureaucracy

Purdy slumped into the arm of the guard, breathing heavily and terrified for the fate of her friends left out on the street.

"Excuse me, Miss" the guard was struggling to hold her and his gun and he planted her into a nearby chair "Are you ok? Do you need medical help?"

"No, no medical help, thank you, I just need to catch my breath. Can you see my friends on the street, are they ok?"

The guard walked over to the door and looked out of the window.

"I don't see anyone anymore, the street is empty" he called over to her.

"Is the car still there?"

"There are no cars at all, all quiet." he said, walking back towards her. He had a Liverpudlian accent, Purdy welcomed the sound of his Beatle-like tones and smiled to herself, if the car was no longer there she had to hope that Fred and Thomas had managed to get away again.

"You're too early for our regular office hours," he informed her "but I could see you were having trouble and I'm not one to leave a lady in distress, thought you should come in and I could make you a brew."

"Thank you, thank you, you are my absolute hero!" she smiled at him "I'm Purdy, by the way, a cuppa would be just lovely, ta!"

"Call me Scouse," he replied "back in a mo."

Scouse stalked off with his gun under one arm and went into a side door to put the kettle on. Purdy sat and took in her surroundings. The building had a beautiful high ceiling and was really quite ornate. On the wall above her in large brass letters it said 'British Consulate General' next to a huge Royal Crest with the lion and unicorn proudly holding up the crown. Just the sight of the crest made Purdy believe that she was safe now, surely they would have to help a citizen in need.

Scouse came back with two steaming mugs of tea, handed one to Purdy and sat in the chair opposite her.

"I used full fat milk and put a spoon of sugar in it for you, you looked like you could do with the boost." he said and gave her a wink. "You don't have to tell me nothing about why you need help but we have a couple of hours to kill if you feel like chatting, I'm a good listener. And I've signed the Official Secrets Act so I can keep me mouth shut too."

Purdy smiled and thanked him. He seemed a nice lad but she didn't have the energy to go too much into things so she just kept it short and sweet and said she'd been dragged into something that was beyond her control and she needed assistance to extract herself from it. Scouse feigned interest but she didn't give him juicy enough details to keep his attention for very long. She asked him how long he'd been stationed here and he told her that it had been about six months and he liked it but he missed English pubs and football matches, Everton was his team. She suggested a couple of places he might find fun to go to in San Francisco where he could get a pint and watch the footie, for which he thanked her gratefully.

"Right, I'd best be getting to me duties. You wait here, they'll be in soon and you can get an emergency appointment to speak to a Consular Agent I expect. It's been nice to meet yous, I'll test out them pubs soon, ta-tah sweetheart!" and off he went with his gun under his arm through another door.

Purdy sat there going over everything in her head, wondering how to explain it all without sounding too much like a lunatic. She looked a little crazy in her outfit of men's sweatpants and sweater, but it was all a hell of an improvement over the yellow or even blue outfits she'd been forced to wear for the last three months. She sat nervously fumbling with her passport as the minutes went by.

Eventually a young man approached her.

"Hi, can I help you?" he asked pleasantly.

"Oh hello, yes please, I need to speak to someone about a problem I've encountered." Purdy stood up and then continued "I'm British, you see."

"I see" the young man smiled "And what was the problem?"

"Well it's a little complicated actually. I've been..." Purdy contemplated how to introduce the conversation gently "kidnapped, I suppose, and I've just managed to escape and now I'm seeking sanctuary here."

"Kidnapped?" the young man raised his eyebrows "Didn't you consider going to the police first?"

"That's a good question, I know. But I don't know who I can trust, you see, the police might be in on it." she realized how this sounded and noted that he looked somewhat bemused by her.

"In on it... right..." he pondered. "Well, we really would urge you to speak to the local police in a matter such as this, you see we are very busy here..."

"NO!" she said firmly, terrified she was about to be dumped out on the street again, she waved her passport in his direction. "I'm British! I need to speak to someone here. Please."

He could tell she wasn't going to leave without a fuss. He took her passport from her and made towards the other side of the room.

"Ok follow me." he said and took her over to a desk where he tapped on a keyboard for an absolute age, obviously inputting her details, a smirk crossed his face as he read the screen, he handed her back her passport. "Oh yes, it looks like Daphne Carer will be free soon, you can speak to her, she's one of the Agents we have here. Please go take a seat again, I'll call you when she's available."

Purdy was relieved she wasn't to be thrown out anytime soon and she returned to the seat she'd been sat in since arriving. After some time the young man came over to her again.

"Ms Carer can see you now, please follow me." they walked together along a corridor and over to a bank of elevators. The elevator door opened and he pressed 11, the elevator rose up to the 11th floor, they got out and walked up another corridor where they came to a door with Daphne Carer's name on it, the young man knocked.

"Come!" came the female voice from within, he opened the door and let Purdy in, then shut it behind her and went back to his desk.

Purdy entered the room alone and walked over to the desk. It was disappointingly corporate looking, she had expected some grand wooden desk and for the lady to be sat in a big leather chair, in reality it looked like a formica office desk with a black office chair behind it and two black fabric chairs in front, much like she'd walked into the lobby of a bank to sit down with one of their advisors. Daphne walked towards her and extended her hand.

"Hello," she said in an over-the-top poshest of posh voices "Daphne Carer, how do you do?"

"Purdy Sinclair, nice to meet you." Purdy shook her hand. Daphne was wearing a red skirt suit with red shoes and matching red lipstick, she looked not unlike a Virgin Atlantic cabin crew member.

"Now, what can we do for you today, Ms Sinclair? Please do sit down. Harris tells me that you've been subjected to a kidnapping attempt, how awful for you."

"Yes..." began Purdy and she sat down in one of the chairs opposite Daphne, where she began to tell her the entire story.

When she had finished Daphne just sat looking at her with a disbelieving expression on her face. She looked at her monitor screen and pressed a couple of the buttons on her keyboard whilst Purdy shifted awkwardly in her seat, knowing how this all sounded.

"It says in your file that you were arrested and convicted for dealing marijuana. You lost your license to practice law, your job and your home. It seems to me that you are blaming others for your own misfortunes and you've made up this whole story in the hope that we will help get you back to the UK, is that correct?"

"What?!" Purdy was astonished, her file said that? "None of that is true! I've never been in any trouble, I've only ever tried a pot brownie once and I've certainly never dealt any illegal drugs. What file is that? I think you have the wrong person..."

"Prudence Louise Sinclair, British Citizen, born in Hampshire, England, lived Buena Vista Park here in San Francisco until she was evicted for non-payment of debts last month, it's all here in the file in front of me, it matches your passport information."

Purdy couldn't believe her ears, those were her details, not only had they stolen her freedom but they'd stolen her identity too, what was she going to do now?

"Yes some of those details are true, except for the drugs conviction and eviction, that is nothing to do with me. I would never do anything like that, I like my career too much. This is all part of plot against me, conjured up by The Facility in order to cover up what they are doing!"

"So, you're telling me that the US government is in on some farcical conspiracy where wealthy individuals are taking people off of the streets to use as organ donors and taking their babies for God knows what and no one knows a thing about it? And so what? The files we have on you are a complete work of fiction? You are such an upstanding member of society that you turn up here at day break, dressed in a baggy sweater and trousers which don't fit you and I'm supposed to believe you over my governmental files which I use day in and day out? And all you have as proof for me is a plaster on your arm which *you* claim is where you were microchipped but your friend, Ben, whose surname you don't know, used a Swiss Army knife to remove it? I'm sorry, Ms Sinclair, do you really expect me to believe all this?" Purdy's heart sank at Daphne's response and she tried to think of how she could convince her of the truth.

"I will swear on anything that it is the entire truth. Why on earth would I walk in here with some tall tale like this if it wasn't true?."

Daphne's eyes narrowed as she contemplated this, she still suspected this was all just a ruse to get a free ride home to the UK. She started to wonder if Purdy was maybe a little mentally unstable. Her thoughts were interrupted by a knock on her door.

"Come!" she called out.

In walked a tall chap with glasses and a pleasant face.

"Daphne, sorry to intrude..." he possessed another extremely posh voice , he clocked Purdy sat in the chair. "Oh I'm sorry, I didn't realize you were in conference."

"Not at all, Colin, come in, come in, let this young lady tell you her story." Daphne was amused and intrigued to see what Colin thought of the unusual tale.

"Oh of course, hello there, Colin Templeton-Smythe, how do you do?!" he smiled and held out his hand to Purdy, he shook it with vigor and sat down in the chair next to her.

"Purdy Sinclair," she said in a despondent tone and prepared to tell her story again. When she had finished Daphne added into the mix the information that she had found in Purdy's file about the drugs which Purdy vehemently denied.

"OK, OK, I understand you are very upset... and yes, well that all sounds terrible for you..." Colin interrupted her denial, she was sure he didn't believe one word of her story, he too would rather believe the governmental files and her heart sank even further. "I am sure we can find someone to able help you with all that. A word, outside if I may, Daphne. Nice to meet you, uh, Purdy was it?"

Purdy nodded, he smiled and got out of the chair, Daphne followed him to the door and they stepped outside together. Purdy strained towards the door to hear their conversation. Through the hushed tones she could make out that Colin was suggesting that Purdy was likely suffering some sort of mental breakdown and that they should take her to the consulate doctor for his opinion. Daphne disagreed and said that protocol would be to just send her to a local hospital for psychiatric appraisal. Purdy panicked, if they sent her back into the outside world she would be vulnerable to being caught once again, she had to get them to keep her here.

Daphne came back into the room and Purdy sat up, pretending that she hadn't been straining towards the door trying to eavesdrop, although it was obvious to both of them that that is what she had been doing. Daphne leant back on her desk in front of Purdy.

"Ms Sinclair, it seems to me that you may have been under some strain recently and I'm concerned for your health. I'm going to have a car take you to a local hospital for an evaluation..."

"No! Please don't" Purdy implored her. "Please don't make me go back out onto the streets, it's just not safe for me."

"I know, I understand," Daphne was tiring of this woman's rantings and just wanted to move her onto someone else's plate now, that could only happen if she got her physically removed from the Consulate. "But it is for your own good, don't worry, I have a nice assistant who will go with you and get you settled there..."

"I won't go!" Purdy was defiant. "You can't make me..."

"I can and I will." Daphne had now lost patience with her completely. "Wait there!"

She stormed out of her office, leaving Purdy sat alone and considering her options. If she just sat here and waited for Daphne to return she was bound to be bundled out into the world again and left in a hospital where anyone with access to her medical records would find her immediately and they would no doubt drug her up and and take her back. She couldn't take that chance. She wasn't a prisoner here, she could just walk out of the front door herself, at least then no one would be taking her anywhere. She was quite close to the Embarcadero, maybe if she could make it to one of the piers she could stowaway on a boat and at least get away from the US. The streets had more people on them now, maybe she could blend more easily. It had to be worth a shot, after all.

Purdy stood up and made for the door. At first she felt like she had to act covertly but then remembered that she came here willingly, she came asking for help, they had no reason to make her stay and in fact might just be glad to see the back of her. Emboldened by this thought she opened the door to Daphne's office onto the corridor with a sense of purpose, she was not hiding away anymore, she'd done nothing wrong.

Just leaving

The hallway was empty, with not another soul around. Purdy closed Daphne's door behind her and walked towards the elevator bank. She pressed the call button and stood waiting, it seemed to take an eternity. She heard footsteps coming from around the corner, again she told herself she was doing nothing wrong but her pulse quickened and she urged the elevator to get there now.

Daphne came around the corner, stomping her red heels with every step.

"Oh, where are you disappearing to?" she asked.

"I just wanted to get some fresh air, that's ok, right? I mean I'm not a prisoner or anything, am I?" Daphne bristled at Purdy's impertinent retort.

"No, you're not a prisoner at all but I thought you wanted my help, you can't just wander around as and when you please, you know, I am very busy and do not have time to chase you around the building!" just then the elevator doors opened and Purdy got in.

"Well don't worry yourself, I've decided I can do without your help anyway." Purdy said curtly and the doors closed.

"Fine!" Daphne raised her voice at the closed doors and stalked back to her office, annoyed to have wasted this much time on this woman already, she would be making a full report of her disgusting behavior on her file immediately.

Purdy leaned against the wall of the elevator and breathed a sigh of relief, she hated confrontation and it had taken all her energy to confront Daphne like that. She pressed the ground floor button and the lift started to move. It came to a slow down at the 9th floor, the door opened and in stepped Scouse, only this time he was in regular street clothes and not his uniform from earlier that morning.

"Hello again!" he said chirpily to her.

"Oh, hi!" she recognized his accent immediately "Sorry, I didn't recognize you out of uniform!"

"I'll avoid the obvious comment about that sounding like you didn't recognize me with my clothes on," he said cheekily with a wink and she felt her cheeks get hot as she smiled back. "Did you get the help you needed? All sorted now?"

"Not exactly..." she said, not wanting to bore him with the long story but it did occur to her that she could maybe get his help if he was on his way out of the building. "Are you knocking off now?"

"Yep, my day is done I'm just off home to my bed." he said as he pressed the button for the 7th floor.

"Oh" she was disappointed he was getting out on a different floor and she desperately searched for a reason to get out with him.

"Do you need a ride anywhere? I've got me car downstairs, I can drop you off if you like?" he asked casually. For once, it seemed, fate was smiling down on her.

"Oh that would be great, thanks!" she said appreciatively whilst she considered where he could take her. At least if she left the building in his car she might not be noticed by anyone who might be waiting outside for her.

"No problem, I just have to get something from the 7th floor first, if you don't mind tagging along."

"Sure!" she said, she loved to see the inner workings of places and liked the idea that she might be getting a behind the scenes look at the Consulate.

The elevator arrived on the 7th floor momentarily. Scouse waited for Purdy to get out the lift first whilst he held his arm against the open door, very gentlemanly she thought to herself.

"It's just down here..." Scouse was saying and she followed him down another corridor, much the same as the one of the 11th floor and really quite disappointing.

She wondered what it was he needed down here and was about to ask when he stopped in front of a door. He opened it and once again, like a gentleman, held it open for her to go into first, she smiled at him and walked through the door. Intrigued she looked around the room and once again it was a dull looking corporate style conference room. But sat at the end of the long table were two people. One she recognized from Daphne's office, it was Colin Templeton-Smythe and the other, whom she didn't recognize, was a woman about the same age as her. She turned to look at Scouse and he smiled and closed the door, remaining outside in the hallway. Panic arose in her, damn it, she'd let her guard down and been suckered in by Scouse and now had no escape.

"Purdy! You don't mind if I call you Purdy, do you?" Colin spoke to her pleasantly.

"No, you can call me whatever you like, although I would appreciate it if you could let me know what it is I am doing here, I was just about to leave." she was in no mood for games and if this woman was the doctor that Templeton-Smythe had suggested to Daphne that she should see then she wanted to be sure she saw Purdy had her faculties about her and was prepared to take care of herself.

"I don't think that's a very good idea, is it? I mean, aren't you on the run from The Facility?" Colin said to her with a smile.

"Yes, yes, I get it, no one believes me, you all think I've lost the plot, and that's fine, I don't need you to believe me, I'll be off now if you don't mind." Purdy went to reach for the door.

"No! Please, wait a moment," Colin stood up from his seat, "I'd like, if I may, to introduce you to Steph Green, the Consul General."

The lady in the other chair stood up and walked over to Purdy, extending her hand.

"Hello Purdy, it's an absolute pleasure to meet you, won't you please come and sit down? Would you like a cup of tea? Something to eat? We have chocolate hobnob biscuits if you would like them?" Steph smiled warmly as she spoke but Purdy was on her guard.

"No thanks, I'm not hungry." she said, she sat down as invited but she was still suspicious of their motives and what she was doing there so she sat as close to the door as she could. Steph went back around the table and retook her seat.

"Now," Colin said in an efficient tone. "First of all I would like to apologize. We would like you to feel welcome here and it is clear you have not been made to feel that way which is our failing and we are extremely sorry about that. I've told Steph as much as I can remember about your experience at the The Facility but she has some more questions. We really could do with your help."

"Wait, what? Are you saying that you believe me now?" Purdy was suspicious, she was waiting for the punchline.

"It isn't that I didn't believe you when I first heard your story, it's just... it's complicated..." Colin began.

"What Colin means to say," Steph interjected "Is that, as I'm sure you can imagine, The Facility is a very well kept secret and is not widely known about. It is not an officially recognized institution"

Purdy squirmed in her chair, it was beginning to sound like Steph and Colin knew all about The Facility and it concerned her what that was going to mean for her, she braced herself for the news that they were sending her back there.

"Daphne does not have high enough clearance to be informed about it and so her reaction was understandable but, frankly, it was blind luck that Colin happened upon your conversation when he did." Steph continued. "It is not her fault, of course, she took the absolutely correct course of action in the circumstances so we are not blaming Daphne for any of this."

"OK..." Purdy was admittedly impressed with Steph sticking up for her staff but still didn't know where this was going.

"Yes, luckily I had been talking to Harris at reception and he mentioned you and your kidnapping story. I've been conducting a covert investigation, under the direction of Steph, into strange disappearances, kidnappings if you will, of people like yourself. So when he mentioned it to me I thought it might be interesting to hear your story."

"Well, a word to the wise then," mused Purdy. "Maybe it would be prudent to direct your reception staff that anyone coming in with a story like mine be directed to you rather than just randomly assigned? Just a thought."

"Noted, although as I said this is a covert operation but I take your point." Colin liked Purdy, she seemed smart and kept her sense of humor even when her world was crashing down around her ears.

"Yes we'll think about that, thanks. Now I would like to hear everything in detail from you but before we go any further it occurs to me that you might be more comfortable if we got you some clothes that actually fit? What would you like? I can have an assistant order something up for you and we will have it delivered within the hour, just say the word." Steph was eying Purdy's outfit and intuition told her that the baggy sweat pants and shirt had likely not been her first choice.

"Sure, just give me a tablet and I'll pick what I want. But before I do that, I just want to understand something. It sounds like you have some knowledge of The Facility already, correct?" they both nodded in agreement. "Have you met others like me? Others who have escaped?"

"No, we've not met any survivors yet, you are the first." Colin replied bluntly, he noticed Purdy recoil. "I mean, we've not had a direct report from anyone who has experienced it first hand, we've just heard information through intelligence reports."

"And when I've given you the information you need, what do you plan to do with me? Will you just send me out onto the street to fend for myself?" Purdy wasn't giving them any information until she was sure what their intentions were.

"Of course not!" Steph seemed genuinely perturbed by that suggestion. "We don't believe it is safe for you to remain here in the US so we're going to repatriate you to the UK. Anywhere you would like to go, we'll arrange for your passage, we'll also give you a new identity. And, in exchange for your assistance both here and potentially on-going from the UK we have been authorized to give you a one off payment of two million pounds. This should also account for the loss of your property here and go someway to making up your loss of earnings. We appreciate that none of this is your fault and, in order for us to try and stop this situation from happening again to someone else, this is a gesture of appreciation for the help you're going to give us."

"How much?!" Purdy was aghast, she was not expecting that.

"If that's not enough, we can discuss terms later. We have a flight going out tonight that we would like to get you on so if you wouldn't mind, I'd like it if we could get more details from you about where the camp is, I understand you escaped by helicopter, bravo by the way that does not sound like an easy feat!"

Purdy grabbed one of the chocolate hobnobs from the plate on the table, took a swig from a bottle of water and settled in to tell her story in full.

The long journey home

Scouse, she quickly discovered, was not actually a regular guard or indeed soldier, his main role was providing close protection for visiting dignitaries, he'd been going off shift this morning after some classified job and just happened to passing the door as Fred and Purdy banged on it. As he had already gained somewhat of a rapport with her he had been assigned to accompany Purdy until she was safely deposited on her flight home. She felt bad as she knew he'd been on night shift but he assured her that he was fine, he'd be able to get some rest and was fully able to take care of them both. She'd never felt so safe as she did in the company of this gentle giant with an automatic weapon concealed under his jacket.

In contrast, Colin Templeton-Smythe was a noble, statuesque figure, who asked thoughtful questions and proved time and again he had a quick wit, a keen mind for detail and a great deal of empathy for Purdy. Despite first impressions, Colin turned out to be an intelligent and thoughtful man who really could not have been any more sympathetic to her desperate situation. She had been agitated by they way he had seemingly dismissed her on their first meeting in Daphne's office and she'd made up her mind on meeting him again on the 7th floor that she was never going to warm to this preposterously posh halfwit, as it turned out, she was to grow extremely fond of both of these two vastly different men assigned to assist her to freedom.

All three of them spent the day in secluded, comfortable quarters within 1 Sansome Street but away from the main consulate, and shielded from any prying eyes. As promised, an assistant bought Purdy some brand new clothes, just as she'd requested, a pair of Citizen for all Mankind jeans, some black Victoria's Secret underwear and a black v neck shirt. Accessorized with a new pair of Ugg sneakers and a blue scarf. She was so happy to be in jeans and a shirt that, unlike the yellow and blue Facility uniform, did not fit perfectly but made her feel more like herself. The black underwear was not as practical as the nude uniform either but she didn't care, it just felt a hell of a lot more normal to have a choice and for fun, she chose something a little more fancy than she'd been forced into for so long.

Over those few hours they went over everything time and again, Colin trying to extract every minor detail of her experience from her, from the night she was abducted from the Augmented Reality Studios to the moment she was safe in Scouse's grip.

She trawled through her sieve like memory trying to recall any tiny detail that might be helpful. They pored over a map together where Purdy tried to piece together where The Facility was based on her recollection of the helicopter flight, less that 24 hours previously.

They were already aware of the Resistance group but had no information about Ben they could share with her, he wasn't an individual they knew of. She was disappointed, she'd been suppressing her thoughts of Ben since she almost broke down in the street after escaping Caz's car. Sure that he was more than capable of taking care of himself, she wasn't worried so much for his safety, Ben could likely find his way out of any difficult situations but her concern was more for her own selfish reasons. She'd felt a real connection to Ben, in the short time they'd spent together she'd felt extremely at ease in his company, in awe of his thoughtful intelligence and impressed by his resourcefulness, it was rare that she met people like that and now the likelihood she would ever cross paths with him again was so slim she felt bereft at the loss of him.

After hours of talking, Purdy took a break. She desperately wanted to turn her phone back on and check to make sure Fred and Thomas were ok. Colin advised against ever turning her phone on again, he promised they would get her a new one. From a practical perspective this was helpful but she realized that her entire life was in some way wrapped up in that phone. It held all of her photographs, all of her conversations with loved ones, all of her work, all of her existence. Her physical being was the only thing she had left, along with memories, some of which she would forever cherish and some she never wanted to recall again. It made her so incredibly sad in the first instance, in some ways Purdy Sinclair was gone forever. And then she felt hopeful, she could in fact start her entire life again, and maybe that wasn't a completely terrible thing, she had been bored after all and she would always have the memories of Purdy Sinclair to comfort her.

Not surprisingly, the Consulate had secure communication systems and after much deliberation and frantic background checks Purdy was allowed to contact Flo. The Facility's messages to Flo had attempted to completely destroy and permanently sever the relationship between the two old friends. In the beginning they informed Flo that Purdy was just too busy with work to talk to her as normal, then when Flo started to send messages saying she was hurt and upset, The Facility had replied on Purdy's behalf basically informing her oldest ally that she really could care less about hurt feelings and Flo really should just get over it. It had caused a rift and Purdy felt lucky that Flo had even taken her call after she heard the whole story from an angry and confused Flo.

Of course, after Flo heard and understood the Purdy's own story from her own lips (after being sworn to secrecy about what she was to be told) she felt nothing but affection for her friend and concern for her welfare. They both cried, laughed and reminisced over the course of the one call.

Flo insisted that she wanted to come to Heathrow to meet Purdy's plane the following day. This was absolutely forbidden by Colin, if she was to assume a new identity, the last thing that he wanted was for her one contact left in England to be there waiting for her at the airport, it was just too risky. He did agree that once she was safely in the country and they had monitored the situation she would in fact be allowed to meet up with Flo, but it took some persuasion to get him to that point and they had to agree to abide by his rules. They were just so relieved that it wasn't an absolute no that they willingly agreed to his terms.

They agreed to have no contact until Colin approved it personally, said emotional farewells to each other and then hung up the call. Purdy was emotionally spent and exhausted. She had been awake for what felt like days and the last 3 months of relaxation was a distant memory. The drugs were still working their way out of her system and her only focus was whether she would manage to make it back to England without further incident.

Her flight was scheduled to leave at 8.35 that evening. She had a brand new passport which said her name was Jane Smith, growing up she had always wanted to have a name which didn't stand out as much as she felt her's did and this one looked just the ticket, she felt it would help her be a little more anonymous, to blend in more to the crowd, and anonymity was something she was looking forward to after her recent excitement.

Colin and Scouse would both accompany her to the airport and arrangements were in place that would allow her to avoid the usual check in desk and boarding areas, as she had no luggage to take with her they were to leave it to the last minute to leave. At 8pm the three of them got into a Consulate car in an underground parking lot, when they pulled out into the street above it was dark and looked even darker through the blacked out windows of the vehicle. Purdy was reminded that she would never see San Francisco in daylight again and watched forlornly out of the windows as she saw the streets for the last time.

"I expect it's sad, isn't it?" Colin's question interrupted her thoughts.

"Hmm? What's that?"

"Leaving behind this city? You've lived here a long time, haven't you?"

"Yes," she turned to look at him. "I've been here for twelve years. I came here looking for an adventure, get out of my humdrum existence and then that adventure in itself became a humdrum existence I suppose."

"It didn't look that humdrum when you ran into me arms this morning." Scouse attempted to inject a little humor into what he thought sounded like a potentially maudlin conversation, they all smiled and Purdy chuckled softly.

"Yup, yup, you're right, not so humdrum in the last 24 hours." she nodded and recalled the desperate run she made into Scouse's arms earlier that day. "It probably won't stop me from complaining again about the next humdrum moment in my existence either!"

"Do you have any plans about what you want to do with your life now? We can help with getting you any background qualifications you need, you don't have to decide now but when you do you just let me know and I'll fix it."

"Anything?" Purdy pondered the possibilities "So if I wanted to be a surgeon…"

"Well no, not quite anything, obviously!" Colin cut her off, he knew she was joking but she made a fair point, he couldn't ethically get her qualifications and background that would endanger lives.

"I guess I have time to think about it. I'm wondering if I should maybe get back in a helicopter again, maybe actually learn some real skills, apparently you never know when you might need it."

"Sounds good, I can always help find you an instructor if you would like, I know a lot of helpful people." Colin informed her.

"I bet you do." she said. "Thank you. If it wasn't for you who knows how I would have fared out there on the streets on my own this morning. I'm so grateful to you both…"

"Don't mention it, yous'll have us all wellin' up here if you don't stop soon." apparently Scouse was not there for the accolades, he was just doing what he does and she respected that. She smiled at them both and nodded, leaned back in the seat and watched out of the window as they hurried along 101 towards the airport.

As they got close to pulling off at the airport it became obvious to Purdy that both Scouse and Colin were concentrating on checking their surroundings to ensure they weren't followed, it hadn't really occurred to her that she was still in danger, until now they'd done a good job of keeping her relaxed and acting as if this was just a run of the mill uber-like trip to SFO. She stayed quiet in a bid not to distract them, to fall at the last hurdle here before she boarded the flight would be unimaginable.

As they pulled into the airport they didn't go the way Purdy was expecting, this put her slightly on edge, she would have expected to go the way she was well versed in, to the International terminal and then departures. They took a road which she'd never noticed before, in the dark it was hard to see where they were going but she soon realized that they were driving onto the pans and right up to the aircraft which she was to board. She could see through the windows that people were already boarding, some in their seats, some putting luggage in the overhead bins, her tummy flipped at the idea she would be on there soon and on her way home, leaving this all behind.

The car came to a stop just by a set of rickety look-ing stairs which led up to the jet bridge, close to where it was attached to the aircraft. One last look all around them and Colin and Scouse nodded at each other.

"OK, good luck, sweetheart, I hope you have a good flight!" apparently Scouse was staying in the car and not walking her up the stairs. She leaned over and gave him a hug.

"Thank you again" she whispered into his ear as she squeezed him tightly.

"Go on, get out of 'ere!" he warmly squeezed her back before gently chiding her and pushing her to-wards the door. She turned to hug Colin too.

"No need, I'm coming up with you." Purdy felt a lit-tle rebuffed but tried to remember they were work-ing here to keep her safe so she followed their lead.

Colin and Purdy got out of the car, out on the tar-mac it was noisy and a cold wind was blowing. Colin beckoned Purdy to follow him up the steps, Scouse kept watch from the car the whole time to ensure her safety. At the top of the steps Colin banged on the door, which was opened immediately by a woman with a high visibility vest and a radio.

"Hello Colin!" she said brightly. "Where's my VIP?"

Purdy appeared from behind Colin.

"Here she is, Purdy meet Sarah, she's going to take care of you on the flight." Sarah smiled a warm, broad smile at Purdy.

"Hello, let's get you on board, shall we, I've saved you a nice quiet corner in First Class."

"Hi, oh thanks!" replied Purdy, a little surprised to be flying first class, she thought Business Class was fancy enough, she'd never tried first class before.

Purdy turned to say goodbye to Colin.

"Erm, yes, well. I'll be in touch." he mustered. "And you have my number so if you need anything you just give me a call and we can sort that out for you. Have a nice flight now."

"Thank you again, you know, for a posh fella you're alright really." she grinned and reached up to hug him, he awkwardly embraced her, he was typically English and felt uncomfortable at the first sign of anything emotional happening in his immediate vicinity but to his credit he managed to squeeze her tightly in return.

"Thanks Sarah, please take good care of her, she's very special." and with that Colin turned and disappeared back through the doorway.

"Come on Purdy, let me show you where your seat is." Purdy followed Sarah onto the plane and was led to a corner of first class, with her own little cabin with a bed and entertainment galore.

Sarah offered her a pair of pajamas, her blood ran a little cold, they were yellow and she gracefully declined the kind offer. She settled in her seat and Sarah brought her a glass of champagne just as the pilot announced for the crew to take their seats. She leaned back in her seat and sipped the champagne as the plane picked up speed on the runway and lifted off the ground.

She watched out of the window as they climbed higher and higher and the plane banked to go northward. She breathed a long sigh of relief, closed her eyes and leaned back into the soft cushiony first class chair, she was on her way home. There had been times in the last 48 hours when she thought this was never going to happen. So many thoughts bustled for space in her head. So many faces ran through her mind like a picture book. Faces of the people she'd only known briefly but who had helped her and been so kind: Gentle Giant Scouse, Intuitive Steph and Intelligent Colin. Those she had known for longer who she could never repay: Handsome Ben, Dearest Fred and Hidden Depths Thomas. These were the people who would help restore her faith in the human race, if people like this still existed, those who will risk their own safety to help another, then all was not lost.

Her mind skipped to the likes of Caz and Nick, just young girls trying to forge their way in an always connected, ever more narcissistic world, and unlike the distaste she had felt for their vacuous conversation just a few hours ago she now felt a little sorry for them, they, like everyone else, were just trying to survive and thrive in this modern world, victims of their own youth and beauty, sadly believing that's all they have to offer the world when likely they had so much more.

For the last three months she had eaten three meals a day with people she knew nothing about. Georgia, Derek and Jenny. She had no idea where they were from, or what they had done before falling victim to The Facility and she feared she may never find out their fates either. She thought of Chuck, his fate already sealed and she mourned for him as she realized no one else likely would or even could mourn for him. Her bitterness towards Jenny had somewhat dispersed too over the course of the day. Jenny was a victim of her own circumstance as well, after all, if choosing to live and work within The Facility was appealing to her, Purdy dreaded to think what life could have been like for her before she made that deal. She mourned for them all in her way and hoped the survivor guilt that she felt was something which would spur her on in the future to try to help as best she could to get these places closed down.

She opened her eyes again in time to catch a glimpse of the iconic bridges out of her window, they were lit up in the darkness just as they always were, a solid, a staple, adding to the skyline that had identified home for her for over a decade and now symbolized a place she could maybe never set eyes on again. The bridges that had stood there so long, that connected this wonderful Peninsula City to the East and to the North. They'd helped guide her way last night in the helicopter and tonight she gave a nod of appreciation towards them both as they flew by.

Six Months Later

Jane sat looking out over the ocean. The evening was getting chilly and she pulled her coat around her. Her two year old labrador, Henry, laid at her feet, he didn't feel the chill as much but he liked to stick close to her, they had become inseparable since Jane had rescued him from a local shelter where he'd been left by a family who'd found him too boisterous for their burgeoning brood. Boisterous, a little bit clumsy and up for adventure, Jane fell for his big brown eyes immediately and as much as she rescued him, he did some rescuing of his own.

Following her harrowing experience at The Facility and this strange new world of Jane Smith she'd been thrown into, she had struggled to adapt. She settled in a small coastal village in the South of England, Colin's people had helped to find her the perfect chocolate box thatched cottage, with a lovely little garden with a stream running through it and an ocean view from the upstairs bedroom. They had installed discreet security for her and constantly monitored her safety from their offices in a City nearby. For the first few weeks Jane was too terrified to leave the house. She had a whole life to create and she kept herself busy decorating, ordering a whole new wardrobe of clothes on line and trying to decide who Jane was and what her tastes were.

Eventually Colin was in contact and said it would be safe for her to meet up with Flo. He arranged it for them, and sent a car to pick Jane up to take her to her friend's house. The reunion was extremely emotional, with Flo's children watching on bemused as to why these two grown women were in tears whilst they hugged each other. Jane stayed with Flo for a week, which gave them the chance to reconnect and for Jane to find some normalcy.

When she returned to her new home she struggled to find purpose with her life and still found few reasons to leave the house. Concerned for her welfare, it was Flo who suggested that Jane find herself a four legged friend, she went with her to the shelter and stood by as she waited for a connection to be made. It was instant when they came across Henry. He was a walking wagging tale, the happiest looking chap in the whole place, his big brown, trusting eyes just begging out for someone to love him. When Jane bent down to stroke him he rested his wide, heavy head with soft floppy ears in her lap and nuzzled his cold wet nose under her hand. She looked at him and she knew, he was the one. Unable to explain how she felt, she just knew, there was a connection, she understood him, he understood her and an unquestioning Flo insisted immediately on gifting him to her by paying the donation to the shelter herself.

Henry moved in and Jane soon got used to having another heartbeat around the place. Henry was smart and cheeky, he made her laugh and he made her feel safe, she had no doubt he would protect her with his own life if he ever needed to. They settled in to life together and Jane regained her confidence. They now went out twice a day for long walks and she had finally found a reason to get out of bed each morning, there seemed like there was purpose in life after all, and it didn't just come from a job, like it had felt it did for so many years.

She didn't miss work, this surprised her somewhat, but maybe she had just had her fill of it, it had once been a great career that she fully enjoyed, but obviously her heart wasn't really in it towards the end and in someways her unexpected "sabbatical" had helped push her in a different direction which she felt more relaxed in. She had time to research things that interested her, to learn again.

She did miss Fred, her heart broke when she realized that she would never be able to contact Fred again. She had insisted that Colin check up that he and Thomas were safe and well and after some investigation he confirmed that they were well and thriving and had experienced no fall out from assisting her in getting to the Consulate that morning. She was relieved that they were well, pleased that it seemed they were still together and still intrigued by mystery man Thomas's background and where his mad driving and covert skills came from, she had to accept she would never know. But she still felt a gaping hole that she no longer had her Fred to hang out with and giggle. She harbored fantasies that Thomas would insist they move to England one day and she would bump into Fred, maybe over an afternoon tea in an anonymous tea shop, just like the ones they had enjoyed so many times before in San Francisco. These fantasies helped stave off the sadness some days but in reality, they couldn't replace the friendship which she missed.

Her other sadness came from her knowledge of The Facility. She couldn't stop having dreams about it and was left with uncomfortable, unanswered concerns about what happened to all the people she met whilst there. Was Jenny really in on it? Did she know what The Facility was? Or was she just as much as victim of the system as the rest of them? Were Georgia and Derek still alive? Where did they come from originally anyway? And what *did* happen to the babies that were born there? Colin had alluded to something which was too horrifying for her to even think about, suggesting that the babies were used for experimenting on or sold, it was to whom they may be sold which haunted her even more so, those poor, unprotected souls, it hurt her heart to think about it and she buried it away deep inside. She had fairly frequent contact with Colin to hear the latest in how they were progressing with getting The Facility and others like it closed down but it was a long, arduous process, with many a twist and turn. She gave as much help as she could and tried not to be a nuisance, her long held hope was that no one else would ever suffer the fate that her fellow inmates had endured.

She stared out over the ocean, mesmerized by the waves as they crashed in against the rocks. She breathed in the fresh, crisp air and thanked her lucky stars she was still there, albeit slightly broken from her experiences, but still able to appreciate and enjoy the world around her.

Suddenly Henry sat up, his heckles up and he curled his lip, letting out a faint growl. Jane jumped and turned her head to see what he had spotted, he reacted this way when he saw rabbits so she wasn't immediately concerned but what she saw when she looked towards where he was facing made her a little nervous. Walking along the cliff top towards her was a lone figure, a man, quite tall, dressed in jeans and a hoodie, with his hands jammed into his jacket pockets. He was wearing a baseball cap down over his ears and had his head down against the brisk sea breeze which was whipping up from the ocean below.

Calm down, there's no need to panic, she told herself. Henry continued to watch the figure and his growling got a little stronger. Jane contemplated telling him to be quiet but was torn, if this man was a danger to her she was grateful for Henry's menacing growl, if he was just some man out for a walk with no interest in her, though, it seemed a little unnecessary to allow her dog to react that way to him. She considered her options. She could get up and walk quickly away or she could just sit and wait for him to pass her.

Jane gripped Henry's lead firmly and made the decision to walk away. She stood up and tugged on the lead.

"C'mon Henry!" she said quietly but firmly to the dog, he resisted a little but realized from her tugging that she meant business and started to walk away with her, although he kept looking over his shoulder at the approaching man.

"Hey!" the man shouted at her.

This spurred her on, and she started to walk faster in the opposite direction. She didn't know anyone here so she couldn't imagine who this man was or why he was shouting out to her. She checked to make sure she still had her scarf and had not left anything behind on the bench which he may be shouting to her about, no everything was accounted for, she pressed on.

"Hey Jane!" he shouted and she froze.

American accent, shit, had they found out her new identity and come for her here? She was tired of running and hiding, maybe she should just stand her ground and let what was inevitable happen. The only thing holding her back from that was her love for Henry, she couldn't bare the thought of him being hurt or left alone. She turned to face her potential assailant with a look of thunder on her face and allowed Henry a slack enough leash to bark loudly at the stranger too.

He took his hands out of his pockets and held them up in a surrender motion, he looked up from under the peak of his cap and Jane took a sharp intake of breath.

"Enough, Henry." she gently tugged on his leash. "Hi."

"Hi, I've been looking for you..." it was the same thing he had said to her in The Facility which had made her heart flip and it sounded as welcome here as it had done there, she smiled back at Ben and wondered whether or not it would be at all appropriate to leap into his arms like a long lost lover right here on her clifftop sanctuary.

45398704R10205

Made in the USA
San Bernardino, CA
07 February 2017